Christopher Pearse Cranch

Ariel and Caliban

With other Poems

Christopher Pearse Cranch

Ariel and Caliban
With other Poems

ISBN/EAN: 9783744773447

Printed in Europe, USA, Canada, Australia, Japan

Cover: Foto ©Andreas Hilbeck / pixelio.de

More available books at **www.hansebooks.com**

ARIEL AND CALIBAN

WITH OTHER POEMS

BY

CHRISTOPHER PEARSE CRANCH

BOSTON AND NEW YORK
HOUGHTON, MIFFLIN AND COMPANY
The Riverside Press, Cambridge
1887

CONTENTS.

CONTENTS.

v

vi CONTENTS.

ARIEL AND CALIBAN.[1]

I.

Before PROSPERO'S *cell. Moonlight.*

ARIEL.

So — Prospero is gone — and I am free —
Free, free at last.   His latest charge have I
Performed with duteous care ; have sent the breeze
To blow behind the ship whose rounded sails
Now bear him homeward ; and I am alone.
Yet I, who pined for freedom — I, who served
This lordly mind, not of my own free choice,
Though somewhat out of gratitude, — for he
By his strong sorcery did release me once
From durance horrible, — now, since the touch

[1] To forestall suspicion of my having borrowed even any sugges-
tion of the idea on which this poem is founded from M. Renan's
" *Caliban* " — though this has a totally different conception from
my theme — I may say that I had written the greater part of my
poem long before I had heard of or seen the brilliant and auda-
cious satire of that distinguished French author.

And sympathy of human souls have warmed
My cold electric blood, and I have known
How sweet it were to love and be beloved
Within the circle of the elements
Whose soulless life is death to human hearts, —
I, here alone, now grieve to be alone,
No longer linked with mortal loves and cares.
For as I flit about the ocean caves,
Or thread the mazes of the whispering pines,
Or in the flower-bells dream long sunny days,
Or run upon the crested waves, or flash
At no one's bidding, but in wild caprice,
A trailing meteor or a thunderbolt, —
Or sing along the breeze that hath no sense
Or soul of hearing, melodies I framed
For Prospero and his child. — I have no will
To work as once, when serving earned this boon
Of liberty, long sought, now tame and cheap.
For what to me are all these air-fed sprites
I marshalled, by his potent art constrained?
Their bloodless cold companionship can give
No joy to me. now half estranged from them.
There 's Caliban, 't is true — a human beast —
Uncouth enough to laugh at — not so vile
Perhaps as he appears —rather misshaped
And thwarted in his growth.   And yet he seems
In this fair Isle, where noble souls have lived,
Like a dull worm that trails its slime along

The full heart of a rose; and now at last
Free from the foot of Prospero, all the more
Slave to himself, crawls feeding where he lists.

Enter CALIBAN *in the distance.*

Lo, here he creeps, and looks as if he meant
To enter his old master's cell.　But no!
I 'll enter first, and there assume the voice
Of Prospero.　He some sport at least shall yield.
Ah, sometimes I must be a merry sprite,
If only to beguile these lonesome hours.

　　　　　　　　　　　　　[*Vanishes into the cell.*

CALIBAN.

So — so — the island 's mine now.　I may make
My dwelling where I choose.　Methinks this cell
Might serve; though somewhat I suspect
Its walls are steeped in magic.　And besides,
Too well my bones remember how that lord
Let fly his spirits at me.　How he cramped
My limbs!　The devil-fish o'ertake his ship!
He 's far away — and I can curse him now,
And no more aches shall follow.　As for him,
Yon drunken fellow — and his mate — good Lord,
How I was fooled to gulp his bragging lies!
The man in the moon, forsooth!　And yet he bore
Brave liquor, though it set my wits agog.
Would there were more of it.　Well, I 'll make my bed

E'en here, where Prosper slept.   King of the isle —
King Caliban!   But I 've no subjects yet,
Save beasts of the wood, and even over them
I lack those strong old charms of Sycorax.

[*Enters the cell.*

ARIEL (*within*).

Halt there !   What man art thou?   Slave — Caliban !

CALIBAN.

Ah, ah!   'T is Prospero back again — Ah me !

ARIEL.

How dar'st thou here intrude upon my rest ?

CALIBAN.

Nay now — I cannot tell — I thought thee gone —
I saw thee go.

ARIEL.

Think'st thou I cannot leap
Across the seas ?   Think'st thou I cannot ride
Upon the wind ?   Know'st thou not Prosper's might?

CALIBAN.

Do not torment me !   Alas, alas, I thought
His book and staff were buried — he at sea !
Ah, here 's a coil — here 's slavery again.
I 'll run, before the cramp gets to my legs.   [*Exit.*

ARIEL (*advancing*).

Good riddance! He 'll not venture here again.
This grot is sacred to remembered forms
'T were base ingratitude could I forget.
Their names make fragrant all the place. They fill
The void of life within me more and more,
And draw me closer to all human-kind.
Much have ye taught me. Thou, O Prospero,
Whom all too grudgingly I served, dost seem
Now not a master, but a gracious friend.
And she — Miranda, peerless in her bloom
Of maidenhood — had I but human been,
What tenderer germs — but no — too late, too late
Those virtues, graces — this proud intellect
That made a sport of magic, and renounced
The sceptre of Wonderland as though it were
The bauble of a child. Too late I see
The topmost glory of the Duke, who shone
Grandest abjuring supernatural gifts —
Most godlike in forgiving his base foes.

(*Pauses in deep thought.*)

There is no life worth living but that life
I missed, the sympathetic interchange
Of mind with mind and heart with heart. This world
Of air and fire and water, where I dwell,
Is but a realm of phantasms — spectral flames
Like the pale streamers of the frozen North ;

Is less than half of life — motion without
Life's warm reality — a trance, a dream.
Nay, even this slave — this son of Sycorax
Hath something human in him.   Might I now
But find some passage to his heart, but breathe
Into his sluggish brain some finer breath,
But lift him to companionship of thought —
'T were worth the trial.   At least I 'll follow him
And wind about him with an airy song.
He 's fond of music, for whene'er I sing
He listens open-mouthed.   He 's not so bad
But some ethereal trap may snare him yet.

(Sings.)

> I, a spirit of the air,
> Now may wander anywhere
> All about the enchanted Isle.
> But no more the master's smile
> Greets me as his door I pass ;
> I shall hear no more. alas !
> Hear no more the magic word
> Of the seer who was my lord —
> > Nevermore !

> Nevermore my flying feet
> Bring him music strange and sweet,
> Run for him upon the wind,
> While the cloven air behind
> Meets with roar and thunder-crack

In the lightning of my track —
Nevermore !

Enter CALIBAN, *listening.*

CALIBAN.

This might be one of them.   Full oft I hear
Their music in the air.   And yet he lies,
And is a devil of Prospero's, for he hints
That Prosper 's gone : and yet I heard his voice.
And yet that voice might be a mimicry.
Good Moon, assist me.   Tell me, friendly Moon,
Is Prospero gone ?   Tell me, good Man i' the Moon,
He will not pinch me again.

ARIEL.

Nay, doubt not, friend.
He 's gone.

CALIBAN.

Now Setebos preserve my bones !
What voice art thou ?   For nothing can I see
But stars, and moonlight twinklings in the woods,
And black broad shadows of the trembling trees,
And here and there a. fluttering zigzag bat.

ARIEL.

I hover in the moonbeam overhead.

CALIBAN.

I think I 've heard thee sing and talk before.
Did Prosper leave thee here to govern us,

And sing us into pitfalls with thy lies
And lying songs?   And yet how sweet thou singest!
Come, show thyself — I think thou 'rt not a fiend.

ARIEL.

I 'll show myself anon.   But do not fear.
Prosper is gone.   A lonely spirit am I
Seeking companionship.   I 'd talk with thee.

CALIBAN

Good — an' thou talkest sense, and wilt not bite
Or hunt me — nor dost bid me bring thee logs.

ARIEL.

I have no need of fuel, nor of food
Nor dwelling, nay, not even of bodily shape.
Yet I can take a shape if so I choose.

CALIBAN.

Then prythee do.   I fain would see thee, friend.
I like it not, this talking to the air.

ARIEL.   .

I 'll humor thee if I can be thy friend.
What shape shall I assume?

CALIBAN.

                    Why, any shape
But Prospero's — and I 'll shake thee by the hand,

And swear thou art as merry a fellow as e'er
I have sat cracking nuts with — in my dreams —
For wide awake I ne'er encountered such.
Nay, this seems like a dream.   Perchance it is —
And I asleep, and babbling in my sleep —
And Prospero still lord of all the Isle.

ARIEL.

Nay, all is real.   I tell thee he has gone.
Follow me now to yonder cave, where laps
The sleepy sea upon the pebbled shore,
Smoothing the flickering wrinkles of the moon,
Who steeps her golden column in the brine.
There will I meet thee in a human garb.

CALIBAN.

Where'er you please, so I but see your face.
You are no Jack-o'-lantern, I believe.
I know thee not, but something tells me true
That I may trust thee.   Sing then.   I will follow.
                              [*Exeunt*, ARIEL *singing.*

SONG.

Follow, follow,
Down the deep hollow —
Down to the moonlit waves,
Down where the ocean caves
The full tides swallow.
Follow, follow !

From the curse, from the blight,
From the thraldom of night,
From the dark to the light,
From the slave to the man
We will lift Caliban.
Farewell, Hecate!   Rise, Apollo!
Follow, follow, follow!

II.

In a cave by the sea. CALIBAN, *and* ARIEL *as a forester, seated.*

CALIBAN.

So then it seems thou 'rt one of these who served
This wizard lord — and he a duke disguised —
One of his tricksy spirits.   I like not this.
Why did'st thou serve him?

ARIEL.

                    He delivered me
From torture by his magic.   I was bound
By gratitude as well as by his spells
To wait upon him.   Oft unwillingly
I served him.   But at last I loved him well;
Knew his soul's greatness, honored what he prized,
Which yet was but his minister — his art;
Felt in my airy veins a blood-warm beat,

Till through them double color seemed to run,
Like moonlight mingled with the rosy dawn.

CALIBAN.

If he was noble. why did he enslave me?
I never did him wrong, till he by force
Took from me this mine island — pent me up
In a vile prison — made me toil and drudge
All day, and when I lagged, beset me sore
With pinches and with terrors of his art.

ARIEL.

Thou nam'st not all he did.   Was he not kind?
Taught thee to speak and reason — treated thee,
At worst, as he would treat a faithful dog,
(For little more thou wast at first.) till thou
Did'st bite the hand that stroked and fed thee. yea,
And would'st have wrought dishonor on his child.

CALIBAN.

I know not.   I was never taught to curb
My passions, and I lived a lonely life.
I wronged him?   Yet my punishment was hard.
I might have served him. yet not been a slave.
It turned all love to hate to be his slave.
He did not treat me as he treated thee.

ARIEL.

I was his servant too.   But I perceived
There was a nearer tie 'twixt him and me,

For which I learned to love him.   Let that pass.
What now behooves thee is to summon up
Thy human heart long styed in ignorance
And fear and hate ; and since thou call'st thyself
Lord of this island, learn to be a lord
In nobler style, and with a human love
Of all things good.   'T were little gain for thee
To have thy freedom, if thou 'rt still enslaved
To baser powers within thee.   What thou hadst
Ere Prospero came, is thine to enjoy and own.
But own thyself — the man within the beast ;
For man thou art, and of the same stuff framed
As his who owned thee — and better than it seemed
Thou wert, perchance, to one whose will enslaved
All human and all elemental power
His magic could enforce, to overpay
For a few brief years the dukedom he had lost.
Learn now to prize thy freedom in a field
Where thou may'st work for good and not for harm.
Curse not, but bless.   If I do chance to talk
Above thy head, I 'll dwarf my thought to thine ;
Or meet thee again when thou upon my words
Hast pondered. . . . Now, by Apollo's shaft, I think
The moon-calf is asleep !   I 'll vanish then.

                                    [*Exit* ARIEL.

III.

Sunrise.

CALIBAN (*waking*).

What, is he gone! Or is it another dream?
It is my fate, I think, still to be duped
With visions and with shows. Perhaps now he
Was the man in the moon — Perhaps we 'll meet
    again.
He may have said the truth. And yet, somehow,
I dropped asleep as when I hear the wind
Sing in the pines, or listen to the fall
Of streams in drowsy summer afternoons.
I do begin to love this spirit — albeit
He spoke in praise of Prosper. Prosper ? — well —
It may be that I knew him not — who knows ?
I am glad he has sailed away though. Setebos!
What — sunrise! Did I sleep so long? In faith
I know it, for I 'm hungry. I will dig
Some mussels from the sand, and pick some fruits.
I 'm not a cub, it seems — said he not so ? —
But made for better things ; no slave — a man
Fit to be talked with, and not called vile names —
Made of the same stuff with that Prospero —
Ah ha! good stuff, do you see ? — the very same —
Only a little soiled. We 'll see — we 'll see.

(ARIEL *sings in the distance.*)

The golden sun the clouds hath kissed
   And fires the hilltops grim and old.
And down the valley melts the mist
   And turns the earth to gold.

The lordly soul is lord of all.
   The heart that loves its human-kind,
Where'er its warming sunbeams fall,
   Leaves night and death behind.

CALIBAN.

Fine sprite, I hear you : think I love you too.
I 'll follow you — though what you said to me
Is hard to understand.   I 'll hear you talk
Again ; but first of all must eat and drink.
Made of the same stuff with that Prospero?
No beast — no slave ! well — this is something new.

IV.

A pine grove by the sea.   ARIEL *as a forester.*

ARIEL.

Free, free at last !   Yet bound by a chain whose links
Are the heart's memories.   Free to roam unchecked,
Untasked.   Free as these glancing dancing waves,
This summer wind.   But by an inward need

Of action, and by late-born sympathies
With human life, bound not the less to serve; —
Though for the present I must waste my art
Upon this son of Sycorax. Yet I have seen
A kindlier sight flash in his brutish eyes,
And in his harsh voice heard a tenderer tone.
I think he almost loves me. But alas,
What room for human fellowship, what hope
To evolve the obstructed and distorted germ
Of manhood here, in idle solitude
Haunted by soulless elves and sprites — a land
By human hearts and human intellects
Untenanted? Around us Nature smiles
In indolent repose — too beautiful,
Too soft — a land of dull lethargic ease,
Steeped in the oblivion of the sleepy South.
> (*Pauses in thought.*)

I know another island — where the North
Blows with a fresher wind; — where pulses bound
Electric to assured results of thought.
Its fertile plains, its rocky coasts and hills
Are peopled with a vigorous race. Its ports,
Forests of masts; its fields by labor tilled;
Its growing towns and cities from afar
Flash in the morning of a crystal sky,
And stud its winding streams like jewels strung
On silver threads : — a people brave and strong,
Yet peaceful, and advancing in all arts,

Science and culture, by wise freedom nursed.
Oft in my master's errands flying north
I have seen it far across the wrinkling waves,
Facing the sunrise like a golden cloud,
And heard the humming of its alien marts.
And thither we might sail — I and this slave
That was — not long a slave when he has known
Contact with men of a superior mould
In bonds of law and human brotherhood.

CALIBAN (*who has been approaching unperceived*).

Good brother Ariel, you are lost in thought.
I know 't is about something wise and good.
Come — don't be glum.   A penny for your thoughts.

ARIEL.

How like you this fair island, Caliban?

CALIBAN.

Oh, well enough — not having known a better.
And yet 't is lonely here — a prison still,
Although our jailer's gone.   And I would fain
See some new faces — not Italian dukes
Or jesters — I have had enough of them —
But like your own, whene'er you let yourself
Be seen, and condescend to talk with me.

ARIEL.

What think you of a voyage from this shore
To another island ? — better far than this,
I needs must think ; a place where men have built
Great cities, tilled broad fields, and sail huge ships —
A home for you and me more fit than this ;
For I 'm becoming human very fast,
While you will need ere long some earthlier friend.

CALIBAN.

Well — on the whole I 'm tired of this dull life,
And don't object to see some other lands :
But how do you propose to sail away
Without a ship ?

ARIEL.

　　　　We 'll see. 　Trust me for that.
One task the more my magic shall achieve.
We 'll build a boat. 　Your toil shall not be great.
Yet your old task you must resume awhile,
And bring me a few logs.

CALIBAN.

　　　　Most willingly
For you, good Ariel. 　But for Prospero —
Thank Heaven, I 've carried my last load for him !

　　　　　　(*They retire, talking together.*)

V.

Sunset. ARIEL *and* CALIBAN *in a sail-boat are leaving the island.*

ARIEL *sings.*

I have built me a magical ship ;
  Its sails of the air were wrought.
From the land of symbol and dream we slip
  To the land of deed and thought :
To a clime where the north and south
  Have mingled their noble seed ;
And the glance of the eye and the word of the mouth
  Are one with the honest deed.
        We sail, away, away !

To a land where the brain of man
  Works magic as strange as this ;
And the heart of the future builds a plan
  As deep as the soul's abyss.
We need not the tide nor the gale,
  Nor the sun nor the moon with their beams,
For our boat has a magical rudder and sail
  That were wrought in the island of dreams.
        Away, away, away !

(*Voices, echoing from the island.*)

In the island of dreams we stay.
We echo your parting lay.
Speed on by night and day!
Speed on! away, away!

(CALIBAN *sleeps.*)

ARIEL.

Sleep on! We leave the past. The night enshrouds
The enchanted isle. And wake thou when the sun
Shines on another clime — and shines in thee
With the new light which thou hast never seen.

L'ENVOI.

Pardon, great Poet, should I seem to mar
  One mystery of thy supernatural tale ;
Or with unreverent eye to scan the star
  Whose splendor makes his satellites so pale!
If in my play and privacy of thought,
  Led by thy light, I lingered for a while
Amid the scenes thy master-hand had wrought,
  And, hovering over thy deserted isle,
  Dared to invoke thy sprites without command
  To come unmarshalled by thy mystic wand —
If on the margin of thy immortal page
I scrawled a sketch unfit to grace thy stage,
  'T was but the joy of dwelling there with thee
    Near that enchanted sea.

'T was but the wondering question of a child,
To know what may have chanced beyond the wild
Fantastic dream, from which too soon he woke
To common daylight and life's weary yoke.
Pardon I crave once more, O mighty seer!
    I bow before thee here
    With reverent love and awe,
And say — "I only sported with his thought,
While in its golden meshes gladly caught,
I dreamed and fancied. He awoke and saw!"

LIONEL AND LUCILLE.

I.

In the beautiful Castleton Island a mansion of lordly
  style,
Embowered in gardens and lawns, looks over the glimmering bay.
In the light of a morning in summer, with stately beauty
  and pride,
Its turrets and glittering roof flash down from the hills
  like a star.
There, pillowed in woods, it blinks on the dusty village
  below ;
And ere it settles itself to its rest in the ambered dusk,
Its windows blaze from afar in the gold of the setting
  sun.

There in a curtained alcove facing a lawn to the south,
Lucille one morning in early spring was sitting alone.
Now in a novel she read, and now at her broidery
  stitched ;
And now, throwing both aside, at her piano warbled and
  trilled.

Then on a balcony leaning, she wished that the weeks
  would pass,
For she with her mother to Europe was going.   Her
  father had died
And left her an heiress; and lovers like moths came
  fluttering round,
Dazzled with visions of gold, and half believing them
  love, —
All but one, who was poor, and loved her, but not for
  her wealth.   .
Three months had Lionel known her — but never had
  told her his love.
How could he ask her to wed him, the scholar who
  drudged for his bread?
Even were his offers accepted, (and little his chances, he
  thought,)
What would they say in the city?   "He has picked up
  a fortune, it seems:
A shrewd lucky fellow!"   So proudly he kept his fond
  thoughts to himself.
Seldom he saw her alone.   In a circle of fashion she
  moved.
Whenever he called, there were carriages waiting, with
  liveries fine —
Visitors going and coming, with shallow and gossiping
  talk.
Those who knew him would surely have said, "'T is
  strange he should love

A girl of such frivolous tastes." But such are the ways
    of the heart —
Ever a riddle too deep for the crude common-sense of
    the world.

To-day no visitors came, and Lucille was deep in her
    book —
(A tale of romantic affection far back in the Orient
    days) —
When a ring at the door was heard, and — Lionel stood
    in the hall.
He had heard she was going to Europe. He would n't
    yet bid her good-bye,
For he hoped he might see her again ere fate put an
    ocean between.
Something more earnest than usual she felt was in
    Lionel's face ;
Something more tender and deep in the tones of his
    tremulous voice,
Though half hidden in jest too grave and intense for a
    smile.
She, brimming o'er with her poets, and fresh from her
    bath of romance,
Clothed the season, and him, and herself, in an opaline
    light.
Softer her tones, and her words less tinged with fashion
    and form,
Cordially lighted like birds on the ground of his intimate
    thoughts.

And as he left her, to stroll on the hills of the beautiful
    island,
Hope with her roseate colors enveloped the earth and
    the sky.

'T was one of those April days when the lingering Winter
    stands
Waving his breezy scarfs from the north for a last good-
    bye ;
When the delicate wind-flowers peep from the matting
    and moss of the woods,
And the blue Hepatica lurks in the shadowy dells of the
    fern ;
When the beautiful nun, the Arbutus, down in her clois-
    ters brown,
Creeps through her corridors damp in the dead old leaves
    of the past,
Whispering with fragrant breath to the bold things dan-
    cing above :
" Tell me, has Winter gone ?   May I peep — just peep,
    at the world ? " —
When the spaces of sky are bluer, with white clouds
    hurrying fast,
Blurring the sun for a moment, then letting him flash
    on the fields,
While the shadows are miles in breadth, and travel as
    swift as the wind
Over the sparkling cities afar and the roughening bay ; —

When the pine-groves sigh and sing as the wind sweeps
    under and through
The cheerful gloom of their spicy shade ; and the wil-
    lows lithe
Bend and wave with the tender green of their trailing
    boughs ; —
When the furry catkins drop from the silvery poplar tree ;
When the bare, gray bushes are tipped with the light of
    their new-born leaves,
And the petted hyacinths sprout and curl their parasite
    lips
Under the sunlit, sheltering sides of the palace walls,
And seem to scoff at the violets hidden deep in the grass,
And the common, yellow face of the dandelion's star,
As it peeps like a poor man's child through the rails of
    the garden fence.

Then, as Lionel entered the crowd and the city again,
Lighter his labors appeared in his office, wall-shadowed
    and dusk.
Dreams of the island and woods swept over his figures
    and books :
Visions of love in a cottage, with fashion and splendor
    forgotten.
Changeable April had shown but its sunniest side to his
    heart.

Once more, — twice. to the island he went : and Lionel
    hoped

A tenderer feeling for him had dawned in the heart of
  Lucille.
Ever with friendlier greeting she met him : for she in
  her mind
Had dressed up a hero of fiction; and Lionel — could
  it be he ?
Was not his name of itself a romance? Then his face
  and his form,
Voice and manners and culture, were just what her hero's
  should be.
So with the glamour of life unreal she saw him; and
  yet —
Was it love? She thought so, perhaps. At least she
  would dream out her dream :
This was a real live novel — and worth reading through,
  was it not ?

II.

One day, when the bushes were white in the lanes, and
  the bees were astir
In the blooms of the apple-trees, and the green woods
  ringing with birds,
Lionel asked Lucille to walk with him over the heights
Looking far down on the Narrows and out on the dim
  blue sea.
So through the forest they strolled. They stopped here
  and there for a flower,
Then sat to rest on a rock. An oak-tree over their
  heads

Stretched abroad its flickering lights and shadows.　The birds

Sang in the woodlands around them.　The spot seemed made for romance.

And Lionel drew from his pocket a book that had lately appeared,

A volume of lovers' verse by a poet over the seas,

And read aloud from its pages.　Lucille sat twisting a wreath,

Laurel and white-thorn blossoms that half dropped away as she twined them ; —

Paused now and then to listen ; and as he was closing the book,

Laid a wild flower between the leaves to remember the place —

And playfully placed her wreath on his head, as if *he* were the poet.

Silent and musing they sat, as they turned to look at the sea,

Watching the smoke of the steamers and white sails skimming afar.

And Lionel said, " Ah, soon *you* too will be steaming away

Down the blue Narrows ; and I — shall miss you — more than you know."

" Why should you miss me ? " she said.　" So seldom you visit our house."

" Had I but followed my wishes ; — but you like the lady appeared,

Shut in the circle of Comus. How hard to enter your
  ring ! "

" What should prevent you from coming ? How often I
  wished you would come !

Nobody calls that I care for : our island is growing
  so dull."

" Yes — and you long for a change — and so you are
  going to Europe.

There in a whirl of delights, with fashion and wealth at
  command,

Soon you 'll forget your poor island, and all the admirers
  you knew."

" No " — she whispered — " not all " — and blushed,
  with her head turned away,

Looked down and murmured : " You think I am wedded
  to fashion and wealth :

Yet often I long for the simpler manners the poets have
  sung,

The grand old days when souls were prized for their
  natural worth.

You think I can rise to no feelings and thoughts of a
  serious life —

Can value no mind and no heart but — such as you meet
  at our house.

I care not for such — I fancied you knew me far better
  than that."

" Lucille " — he never had called her Lucille, but the
  name came unbidden ;

" Lucille, could you love a poor toiler who dared not to
offer his heart
And his hand — and in silence had loved you, and
wished you were poor for his sake,
So fortunes were equal ? " And she, still floating in rosy
romance,
Murmured, " I could," with a look that melted the walls
of reserve
And mingled two souls into one. Then, turning away
from the sea,
The sea that so soon must divide them, they pledged to
each other their troth.
And Lionel saw not the fates that were frowning afar
o'er the waves ;
For the world wore the color of dreams, as homeward
they wended their way.

Bright were the meetings that followed — and yet with
a shadowy touch
On Lionel's hopes, as if in the changeable April days
He still were roaming the hills, and still looked over the
bay
Where cloud and sunshine were flying, with doubtful
promise of spring.
Lucille had a reason, it seemed, to keep their betrothal
untold.
The day was so near of their parting. She feared what
her mother might say.

'T were best they should part but as friends. They would
    write to each other the same —
And they would be true to each other — and all would
    be clear before long.
And Lionel yielded, and pondered.   And so they parted
    at last.

III.

The summer had hardly begun when a letter from Eng-
    land came,
Full of the voyage and landing — but little of what he
    had hoped.
Too light, too glancing it seemed for a first love-letter
    from one
Far over the sea, who had said he should ever be first
    in her thoughts.
Bright and witty it fluttered from topic to topic — but
    never
Paused with a tremulous wing to dwell on the love she
    had left.
Something there was in its tone that said " I am happy
    without you : "
Something too little regretful — too full of her glittering
    life.
And as one gathers a beautiful flower ne'er gathered be-
    fore,
Hoping a fragrance he misses, and yet half imagines he
    finds —

Wooing the depths of its color too rich for no perfume
  to match —
So seemed her letter to him, as he read the lines over
  and over.
Yet when Lionel answered, he breathed not a word of
  the thought,
Shading the glowing disc of his love with distant surmise.
"Soon," he said, "will the novelty cease of this foreign
  excitement.
Then she will think sometimes of me as the sun goes
  down
Over the western waves — and tenderer tones will flow,
And mingle with warmer words in her letters from over
  the sea."
Yet when another letter came, it brought her no nearer,
Less of herself, and more of the colors that tinted her life.
And Lionel wrote with passionate words : "Only tell
  me, Lucille,
Tell me you love me — but one brief line — and I will
  not complain."
Restless, troubled, one day he passed her house on the
  island ;
Shut to the sun and the breeze, it blinked on the village
  below.
Over the balcony leaned a purple Wisteria vine,
(Blooming, but not in its season, as oft 't is their habit to
  do,)
Trailing its ladylike flounces from window and carved
  balustrade.

And dropping its blossoms as brief as love.   And Lione
 muttered :

" She too over that balcony leaned one day as I passed —
Leaned like a flowery vine; and smiled as I passed be
 low,
And waved me an airy kiss, with a pose of her beautiful form.
Can love that promised so truly be frail as these clus-
 ters of June ? "

Month after month now passed.   Though he wrote as
 fondly as ever,
Brief were her answers, and longer between — till they
 finally ceased.
A year from the day when they parted, a letter from
 Paris arrived,
Short and constrained.   It said: " I fear I have made
 you unhappy.
We have read too much of the poets.   Our troth was a
 thing of romance.
My mother forbids it, it seems.   There are reasons 't were
 painful to tell.
I 'm sure you would find me unfitted — and I am not
 worth your regretting.
Adieu — and be happy.   Lucille."
      Next month in the papers he saw
She had married a Count — some Pole with an unpro-
 nounceable name.

SAN BORONDON.

Saint Brandan, a Scotch abbot, long ago
Sailed southward with a swarm of monks, to sow
The seeds of true religion — nothing else —
Among the tribes of naked infidels.
And venturing far in unknown seas, he found
An island, which became monastic ground.
So runs the legend.   Little else was known
Of him we Spaniards call San Borondon.
Some said he was a sorcerer, some a priest ;
None truly knew.   But this is clear at least,
That there was seen to appear and disappear
An island in the west, for many a year,
That bore his name : but no discoverer yet
His feet upon that shore had ever set.

At Teneriffe and Palma I was one
Who saw that island of San Borondon.
A hundred of us stood upon the shore,
And saw it as it oft was seen before.
The morn was clear ; and westward from the bay
It glimmered on the horizon far away.

We watched the fog at sunrise upward curl
And float above that land of rose and pearl;
And sometimes saw behind a purple peak
The sun go down.   And some said, " We will seek
Westward, until we touch the fairy coast,
Or prove it only some drowned island's ghost" —
But after many days returned to swear
The vision vanished in the pale blue air.
Yet still from off the fair Canary beach
Lay the strange land that none could ever reach.
Then others sailed and searched : and some of these
Returned no more across the treacherous seas ;
And no one knew their fate.   Until at last
We hailed a caravel with shattered mast
Toiling to harbor.   Half her sails were gone.
" Ho, mariners, what news of Borondon ? "
We shouted — but no answering voice replied ;
No sailors on her gangway we descried ;
Her shrouds looked ghostly thin, her ropes were dim
As spiders' webs athwart a tree's dead limb;
And still as death she drifted up the bay,
A battered hulk grown dumb and old and gray.
At length she touched the strand, and out there crept
A haggard man, who feebly toward us stepped,
And answered slowly, while we brought him food
And wine.   He sitting on a stone, we stood
An eager crowd around him, while we sought
What news he from San Borondon had brought.

With eyes that seemed to gaze beyond the space
Of sea and sky — with strange averted face,
And voice as when some muttering undertone
Of wind is heard, when sitting all alone
On wintry nights, we see the moon grow pale
With hurrying mists — he thus began his tale.

" We saw the island as we sailed away.
It glimmered on the horizon half that day.
But while our caravel still westward steered,
Amazed we stood — the isle had disappeared.
At night there came a storm.   The lightning flashed
From north to south.   The frightful thunder crashed.
Under bare poles we scudded through the dark,
Till morning gleamed upon our drifting bark —
The red-eyed morn 'neath beetling brows of cloud, —
And the wind changed.   Then some one cried aloud,
' Land — at the westward ! '   And with one accord
All took contagion of that haunting word
' San Borondon.'   The island seemed to lie
Three leagues away against a strip of sky
That on the horizon opened like a crack
Of yellow light beneath the vault of black ;
Then, as with hearts elate, we nearer sailed,
The clouds dispersed, the sun arose unveiled.
The wind had almost lulled ; the waves grew calm.
We neared the isle, we saw the groves of palm,
The rugged cliffs, the streamlet's silver thread

Dropped from the misty mountains overhead ;
The shadow-haunted gorges damp and deep ;
The flowery meadows in their dewy sleep ;
The waving grass along the winding rills ;
And, inland far, long slopes of wooded hills.
And all the sea was calm for many a mile
About the shores of that enchanted isle.
Our sails half-filled flapped idly on the mast ;
And all the morning and the noon had passed
Before we touched the shore.   Then on the sand
We stepped and took possession of the land
For Spain.   No signs of life we heard or saw.
But suddenly we stopped with fear and awe ;
For on the beach were giant footsteps seen,
And upward tracked into the forests green,
Then lost.   But there, with wondering eyes we found
A cross nailed to a tree — and on the ground
Stones ranged in mystic order — and the trace
Of fire once kindled in that lonely place.
As though some sorcerer's sabbath on this ground
A place for its unholy rites had found.
And so, in vague perplexity and doubt,
Until the sun had set, we roamed about.
And some into the forest far had strayed,
While others watched the ship at anchor laid.
When through the woods there rang a distant bell.
We crossed our breasts, and on our knees we fell.
Ave Maria — 't was the hour of prayer.

A consecrated stillness filled the air.
No heathen land was this; no wizard's spell
The clear sweet ringing of that holy bell.
Scarce had we spoken, when we heard a blast
Come rushing from the mountains, fierce and fast
Down a ravine with hoarse and hollow roar;
And sudden darkness fell upon the shore.
'The ship — the ship! See how she strains her rope —
All, all aboard — cast off! we may not hope
To save her on these rocks. Away, away!'
Then as we leapt aboard in tossing spray,
Still fiercer blew the wind, and hurled us far
Into the night without a moon or star.
And from the deck the sea swept all the crew.
And I alone was left, to bring to you
This tale. When morning came, the isle was gone —
The unhallowed land you call San Borondon;
A land of sorcery and of wicked spells,
Of hills and groves profane and demon dells.
Good friends, beware! Seek not the accursed shore,
For they who touch its sands return no more,
Save by a miracle, as I have done —
Praised be Madonna and her blessed Son!"

Such was his story. But when morning came,
There lay that smiling island, just the same.
And still they sail to find the enchanted shore
That guards a fearful mystery evermore.

A thousand years may pass away — but none
Shall know the secret of San Borondon.

And so, perchance, a thousand years may roll,
And none shall solve the enigma of the soul —
That baffling island in the unknown sea
Whose boundless deep we name Eternity.

THE OLD YEAR.

O GOOD Old Year ! this night 's your last.
And must you go ?   With you I 've passed
    Some days that bear revision.
For these I 'd thank you, ere you make
Your journey to the Stygian lake,
    Or to the fields Elysian.

Long have you been our household guest ;
To keep you we have tried our best.
    You must not stay, you tell us,
Not even to introduce your heir,
Who comes so fresh and debonnair
    He needs must make you jealous.

I heard your footsteps overhead
To-night — and to myself I said
    He 's packing his portmanteau.
His book and staff like Prospero's
He has buried, where nobody knows,
    And finished his last canto.

Your well-known hat and cloak still look
The same upon their entry hook,
　　And seem as if they grew here.
But they, ah me ! will soon be gone,
And we be sitting here alone
　　To welcome in the New Year.

The boots so oft put out at night
Will vanish ere to-morrow's light
　　Across the east is burning.
When morning comes, full well I know
They 'll leave no footprints in the snow
　　Of going or returning.

At twelve o'clock to-night Queen Mab
Will take you in her spectral cab
　　To catch the downward fast train.
Some of us will sit up with you,
And drink a parting cup with you,
　　While I indite this last strain.

O good old wise frost-headed Year,
You 've brought us health and strength and cheer,
　　Though sometimes care and sorrow.
Each morn you gave us newer hope
That reached beyond the cloudy scope
　　Of our unseen to-morrow.

We knew you when you were, forsooth,
No better than a stranger youth —
    A *fast* youth, some one muttered,
When thinking how the days you gave
On ghostly horses to their grave
    Have galloped, flown and fluttered.

But what is time, by moon and stars
Checked off in monthly calendars,
    To fairy kings like you here ?
What are the centuries that span
The inch-wide spaces ruled by man ?
    Or what are Old and New Year ?

You go to join the million years,
The great veiled deep that never clears
    Before our mortal seeing :
The shrouded death, the evolving life,
The growth, the mystery, the strife
    Of elemental being.

We see in your abstracted eye
The clouded flame of prophecy,
    Of time the immortal scorning —
And yet the sympathetic smile
That says, " I fain would stay awhile
    To bid your rhymes good-morning."

Ah! no more rhymes for you and me,
Old Year, shall we together see, —
    Yes, we to-night must sever.
Good-bye, old Number Seventy-five!
It 's nearly time you took your drive
    Into the dark forever.

The train that stops for you will let
A stranger out we never met,
    To take your place and station.
With greetings glad and shouts of joy
They 'll welcome him — while you, old boy,
    Depart with no ovation.

Besides, he has a higher claim
Than you — a grand ancestral name
    That sets the bells a-ringing.
The great Centennial Year is he.
The nation's noisy jubilee
    Young Seventy-six is bringing.

I hear the puffing of his steam.
I hear his locomotive scream
    Across the hills and meadows.
One parting glass — the last — the last!
Ten minutes more. and you 'll have passed
    Into the realm of shadows.

Five minutes yet ?   But talk must end.
On with your cloak and cap, old friend !
    Too long we have been prating.
Your blessing now !   We 'll think of you.
Ah, there 's the clock !   Adieu — adieu !
    I see your cab is waiting.

December 31, 1875.

THE CENTENNIAL YEAR.

A HUNDRED years — and she had sat, a queen
Sheltering her children, opening wide her gates
To all the inflowing tribes of earth.   At first
Storms raged around her; but her stumbling feet
Were planted firm upon the eternal rock.
Her young majestic head with sunny curls
And features tense with hope and prophecy
Now rose above the clouds of war.   She gazed
Wistful yet calm into the coming years,
And grew in strength and wisdom : and afar
Across the sea the nations of the world
Beheld, and muttered from their ancient halls,
" Who is this stranger, young, unskilled and bold,
This Amazonian regent of the wilds
We spurned, and only sought when exile doomed —
Whose sons are marshalling the land and sea,
The winds, the electric currents and the light,
To do her bidding ?   Who this Titan queen
Whose face is flushed with sunrise, and whose hands
Reach forth to welcome all our swarms disowned,
Cast forth upon her shores, and turn their blight
To bloom and culture — e'en their crime to good ? "

Then some beheld her with derisive sneers,
Judgments derived from rules of use outworn,
And stale conventional comparison ;
With fear and envy some — others with awe
And vague hope of ideal rights of man, —
Green harvests now, but swelling into grain
For future time.
            And still the years rolled on.
Tremors of battlefields thrilled through her limbs,
Once, twice, and thrice — the last, alas ! like shocks
Of agonizing pain ; for round her feet
Her own — her children grappled in the fields
Of blood and cannon-shot and fire and smoke —
One recreant multitude for slavery's crown,
And one for freedom and the common cause
That gave the country birth, and pledged the States
To unbroken union based on equal rights.
But justice triumphed, and the stricken land
Regained her poise hard-won.
            Still rolled the years,
Till now she rounds her circling century ;
And Peace and Plenty smile upon her fields
That stretch from sea to sea.   Then she arose
And spake unto the States that clustered round,
Her children all, war's yawning gulf o'erbridged,
North, south, and east and west, her children still ;
And to the ancestral realms across the seas : —
" This year I celebrate my birth.   For me,

One of the Titan race of latest days,
A race Saturnian fables knew not of,
When giants grew, but hearts and minds were dwarfed
And cramped by precedents of brutal force
That stormed Olympus, so must needs be crushed —
For me a hundred years are as one year
To you, and this centennial year a day.
Therefore 't is meet that we invite the world
To bring its various treasures to our shores,
And blend with us, through symbols and results
Of art and grand achievement, in the creed
Of human brotherhood.   And may this year
Be as the seal and pledge of race with race
Forever — one with all, and all with one ! "

Then in a chosen spot, where the first vows
Of Liberty were plighted, we beheld
A wonder-work, as though some Geni snared
By incantation wrought the people's will.
For stately palaces arose and gleamed
Amid the trees ; and on the distant sea
Came argosies full-laden with a wealth,
Not such as Cortez from the plundered realms
Of Montezuma bore, blood-steeped and wrapped
In crime, back to voracious Spain — but brought
With friendly rivalry from every clime ;
From shops and looms of quiet industry
And rare inventive art ; more wonderful

Than crude barbaric days could ever dream.
There, heaped profusely through those spacious halls,
The treasures of the abounding century
Were ranged in order. Thither, as to a shore,
The crowding time-waves of a hundred years —
Silent as streams of air — had pulsed and flowed
And broke in surges, not of yeasty foam,
Resultless thought, and aimless bubble-dreams,
But products of the busy world-wide Mind.
From European and from Asian lands,
From tropic heats and Arctic solitudes,
From towns of traffic and from western wilds,
From sunless mines and clear, high-windowed halls
Of skill and industry, and lonely rooms
Where artists and inventors dreamed and toiled,
Pledged to some dear thought-burden of a life : —
From schools and laboratories closely bent
On nature's inmost secrets, and where swift
Discovery trod upon discovery's heels,
In silent unforeseen audacity
Of masterly conception and result.
Here Europe lavished all her modern wealth
Of apt contrivance, imitative skill,
And costly comfort. There remote Japan
With strange and fascinating styles of art
Took fancy captive ; and the Orient lands,
Whose more familiar forms we knew. set forth
Their porcelain wonders and their bronzes quaint.

Their ivory lace-work and their brilliant silks.
And there, from end to end of one vast space
Throbbed the blind force whose swift gigantic arm
A thousand glistening iron slaves obeyed,
By science taught to serve the age's need.
And day by day the thronging multitudes,
Flowing and ebbing like a tide, swept by,
And up and down through halls and corridors
Feasting their eyes in endless holiday,
Through long, far-reaching vistas all compact
Of use and beauty.

                Proud she well may be.
Once cast on rocks and cradled in the winds,
She now commands, our Titan mother queen ;
While thus the flattering world crowds round her feet,
One half to see the gifts the other half
Has laid before her — and we celebrate
Her first proud century's close with worthy signs
Of universal brotherhood and peace.

Then ring, ye bells ! and let the organs blow
And swell the choral hymn of praise and joy.
And let the grand orchestral symphonies
Resound through park and palace ; while afar
The flying thunders of the steam bring in
And out the thousands who in joyous groups
Make blithe centennial festival and cheer.
And as the autumn days move calmly on,

And from the trees the red and yellow leaves
Drop to the earth — let not the lesson fall
Unheeded.   With fraternal grasp we have met
Through all these summer and autumnal months.
Henceforth may peace and unity prevail
O'er all the land.   America demands
No pledge less true for her Centennial Year.

October, 1876.

AFTER THE CENTENNIAL.

(A HOPE.)

BEFORE our eyes a pageant rolled
  Whose banners every land unfurled;
And as it passed, its splendors told
  The art and glory of the world.

The nations of the earth have stood
  With face to face and hand in hand,
And sworn to common brotherhood
  The sundered souls of every land.

And while America is pledged
  To light her Pharos towers for all,
While her broad mantle, starred and edged
  With truth, o'er high and low shall fall;

And while the electric nerves still belt
  The State and Continent in one, —
The discords of the past shall melt
  Like ice beneath the summer sun.

O land of hope! thy future years
  Are shrouded from our mortal sight;
But thou canst turn the century's fears
  To heralds of a cloudless light!

The sacred torch our fathers lit
  No wild misrule can ever quench;
Still in our midst wise judges sit,
  Whom party passion cannot blench.

From soul to soul, from hand to hand
  Thy sons have passed that torch along,
Whose flame by Wisdom's breath is fanned,
  Whose staff is held by runners strong.

O Spirit of immortal truth,
  Thy power alone that circles all
Can feed the fire as in its youth —
  Can hold the runners lest they fall!

      February 2, 1877.

A NIGHT-PICTURE.

A GROAN from a dim-lit upper room —
A stealthy step on the stairs in the gloom —
A hurried glance to left, to right
In the court below — then out in the night
There creeps a man through an alley dim,
Till lost in the crowd.   Let us follow him.

The night is black as he hurries along;
The streets are filled with a jostling throng;
The sidewalks soak in the misty rain.
He dares not look behind again —
For every stranger eye he caught
Was sure to know his inmost thought.
The darkened casements looking down
From tall grim houses seemed to frown.
The globes in the druggists' windows shone
Like fiery eyes on him alone,
And dashed great spots of bloody red
On the wet pavements as he fled.
And as he passed the gas-lamps tall,
He saw his lengthening shadow fall

Before his feet, till it grew and grew
To a giant self of a darker hue.
But turning down some lampless street
He left behind the trampling feet,
And on through wind and rain he strode,
Where far along on the miry road
The unwindowed shanties darkening stood —
A beggarly and outlawed brood,
'Mid half-hewn rocks and piles of dirt —
The ragged fringe of the city's skirt.
Then on, still on through the starless night,
Shrinking from every distant light,
Starting at every roadside bush,
Or swollen stream in its turbid rush —
On, still on, till he gained the wood
In whose rank depths his dwelling stood.
Then over his head the billows of wind
Rocked and roared before and behind ;
And all of a sudden the clouds let out
Their pale white moon-shafts all about
A dreary patch where the trees were dead,
By a rocky swamp and a ruined shed ;
And a path through the tangled woods appeared
Between two oaks where the briers were cleared.
And under the gloom he reaches at last
His door — creeps in and locks it fast ;
Then strikes a match and lights a lamp,
And draws from his pocket heavy and damp

A wallet of leather thick and brown.
Then at a table sitting down,
To count the — Hark, what noise was that!
A rattling shutter? A rasping rat
Under the floor? He turns to the door,
And sees that his windows are all secure.
Then kindles a fire, and dries his clothes,
And eats and drinks, and tries to doze.
But down the chimney loud and fast
Like distant cannon roars the blast,
And on the wind come cries and calls
And voices of awful waterfalls,
And winding horns and ringing bells,
And smothered sobs and groans and yells.
And though he turns into his bed
And wraps his blanket around his head,
Sleep will not come, or only sleep
That slides him down on an unknown deep,
From which he starts — and then it seemed
He had not done the deed, but dreamed.
Ah, would it were a dream, the wild
Wet night, and he once more a child!

  . . . .

On a flying train, in the dawning day
And the fragrant morn, he is far away.
But secret eyes have pierced the night,
And lightning words outstripped his flight.
And far in the north, where none could know,
The law's long arm has reached its foe.

A CHILD-SAVIOR.

(A TRUE STORY.)

SHE stood beside the iron road,
   A little child of ten years old.
   She heard two meeting thunders rolled
From north and south, that plainly showed
   Danger too fearful to be told.

Nearer, still nearer, rumbling on,
   One train approached with crashing speed.
   What could she do?   Who would give heed
To her — a child, who stood alone
   And voiceless as a roadside weed?

A feeble cry she raised, and stood
   Across the track, — and then untied
   Her little apron from her side,
And waved it swiftly as she could —
   If only she might be espied!

If only on the hissing back
  Of that huge monster nearing fast
  The engineer his eye might cast
On her there on the curving track,
  And heed her signal ere he passed!

, She stands with shout and warning beck;
  On comes the train with thundering roar.
  The fireman sees — he looks once more —
He sees a little waving speck,
  And slackening, slower moves and slower.

"Hi — little girl! what 's all this row?"
  "Another train! — my ears it stuns!
  It rounds the curve like rattling guns!
Back — back! — for I must signal now
  The other."   And away she runs.

So by this little maiden's hand
  Were hundreds saved from fearful lot.
  But when with awe they spoke of what
They had escaped, and made demand
  About the child, they found her not.

For she had vanished through the wood.
  None guessed her dwelling-place or name,
  Nor by what wondrous chance she came;
While home she ran in blithesome mood,
  Nor knew she had done a deed of fame.

But in the old times they would have said
  It was an angel had stood there —
  The hood above her golden hair
A nimbus glowing round a head
  With supernatural radiance fair.

The small white apron that she waved
  Across the dangerous iron track
  To warn the rushing engines back,
Might have been wings, whose flashing saved
  Five hundred souls from mortal wrack.

  November, 1882.

AN OLD UMBRELLA.

An old umbrella in the hall,
Battered and baggy, quaint and queer;
By all the rains of many a year
Bent, stained, and faded — that is all.
Warped, broken, twisted by the blast
Of twenty winters, till at last,
Like some poor close-reefed schooner cast,
All water-logged, with half a mast,
Upon the rocks — it finds a nook
Of shelter on an entry hook: —
Old battered craft — how came you here?

Ah, could it speak, 't would tell of one —
Old Simon Dowles, who now is gone —
Gone where the weary are at rest;
Of one who locked within its breast
His private sorrows o'er his lot,
And in his humble work forgot
That he was but a toiling bark
Upon the billows in the dark,
While the brave newer ships swept by

Sailing beneath a prosperous sky,
And winged with opportunities
Fate had denied to hands like his.

A plain, old-fashioned wight was he
As these sport-loving days could see ;
He in his youth had loved and lost
His loyal true-love.   Ever since
His lonely life was flecked and crossed
By sorrow's nameless shadow-tints.
Yet never a murmur from his lips
Told of his darkened soul's eclipse.
I often think I still can hear
His voice so blithe, his tones of cheer,
As, dropping in to say "good-day,"
He gossiped in his old man's way.
And yet we laughed when he had gone.
We youngsters could n't understand —
No matter if it rained or shone,
He held the umbrella in his hand.
Or if he set it in the hall,
Where other shedders of the rain
Stood dripping up against the wall,
His was too shabby and too plain
To tempt exchange.   All passed it by,
Though showers of rain were pouring down
And all the gutters of the town
Were torrents in the darkening sky.

He never left it once behind
Save the last time he crossed our door.
Oblivious shadows o'er his mind
Presaged his failing strength.   Before
The morning he had passed away
In peaceful sleep from night to day.
And here the old brown umbrella still
In its old corner stays to fill
The place, as best it may, of him
Who on this wild and wintry night
Is surely with the saints of light —
For whom my eyes grow moist and dim
While I this simple rhyme indite.

TO IONE.

ALL day within me, sweet and clear
  The song you sang is ringing.
At night in my half-dreaming ear
  I hear you singing, singing.

Ere thought takes up its homespun thread
  When early morn is breaking,
Sweet snatches hover round my bed
  And cheer me when awaking.

The sunrise brings the melody
  I only half remember,
And summer seems to smile for me,
  Although it is December.

Through drifting snow, through dropping rain,
  Through gusts of wind, it haunts me.
The tantalizing old refrain
  Perplexes, yet enchants me.

The mystic chords that bore along
  Your voice so calmly splendid,
In glimmering fragments with the song
  Are joined and vaguely blended.

I touch my instrument and grope
  Along the keys' confusion,
And dally with the chords in hopes
  To catch the sweet illusion.

In vain of that consummate hour
  I court the full completeness,
The perfume of the hidden flower,
  The perfect bloom and sweetness.

Of strains that were too rich to last
  A baffled memory lingers.
The theme, the air, the chords have passed ;
  They mock my voice and fingers.

They steal away as sunset fires
  Lose one by one their flashes,
And cheat the eye with smouldering pyres
  And banks of gray cloud-ashes.

And yet I know the old alloy
  That dims and disentrances
The golden visions and the joy
  Of hope's resplendent fancies

Can never touch that festal hour
  In soul and sense recorded,
Though scattered rose leaves from your bower
  Alone my search rewarded.

The unconnected strains alone
  Survive to bring you nearer,
As when our queen of song and tone
  Made vassals of each hearer.

Yet through the night and through the day
  The notes and chords are ringing.
Their echo will not pass away —
  I hear you singing — singing.

AFTER–LIFE.

O BOON and curse in one — this ceaseless need
    Of looking still behind us and before!
Gift to the soul of eyes that cannot read
    Life's open book of cabalistic lore ; —

Eyes that discern a light and joy divine
    Twinkling beyond the twilight clouds afar,
Yet know not if it be the countersign
    Of moods and thoughts, or some eternal star.

What taunt of destiny still stimulates
    Yet baffles all desire, or wise or fond,
To pierce the veil ne'er lifted by the fates
    Between the life that ends and life beyond?

We sit before the doors of death, and dream
    That when they ope to let our brothers in,
We catch, before they close, some flitting gleam
    Of glory where their after-lives begin.

And with the light a transient burst of song
  Comes from within the gates that shut again
Upon our dead.   Then we, the proud, the strong,
  Sit crushed and lonely in our wordless pain.

Weeping, we knock against the bars, and call,
  " Speak — speak, O love, for we are left alone ! "
We hear our voices echo against the wall,
  And dream it is a' spirit's answering tone.

" Come back, or answer us ! "   In vain we cry.
  Naught is so near as death, so far away
As life beyond.   They only know who die :
  And we who live can only guess and pray.

If 't were indeed a voice not born within —
  Some sure authentic sign from unknown realms —
Some note that heart and reason both could win —
  Some carol like yon oriole in the elms ;

Though but a vague and broken music caught,
  Heard in the darkness, and then heard no more —
Sinking in sudden silence — while in thought
  We piece the strains outside the muffled door

That leads into the light and perfect joy
  Of the full concert — then 't were bliss indeed
No present griefs could darken or destroy ;
  Somewhere life's mystery we should learn to read.

Somewhere we then might drop the ripened seed
Of life, to grow again beyond the sky —
Nor deem the human soul a withering weed
Born but to bloom a summer time and die.

PRINCE YOUSUF AND THE ALCAYDE.

A MOORISH BALLAD.

In Grenada reigned Mohammed,
   Sixth who bore the name was he ;
But the rightful king, Prince Yousuf,
   Pined in long captivity :

Yousuf, brother to Mohammed.
   Him the king had seized and sent
Prisoner to a Moorish castle,
   Where ten years his life was spent.

Ill and feeble, now the usurper
   Felt his death was hastening on,
And would fain bequeath his kingdom
   And his title to his son.

Calling then a trusty servant,
   He to him a letter gave —
" Take my fleetest horse, and hasten,
   If my life you wish to save.

" Hie thee to the brave Alcayde
  Of my castle by the sea ;
To his hands give thou this letter,
  And his physician bring to me."

Then in haste his servant mounted,
  And for many a league he rode,
Till he reached the court and castle
  Where the captive prince abode.

There sat Yousuf and the Alcayde
  In the castle, playing chess.
" What is this ? " the keeper muttered.
  " Some bad tidings, as I guess."

Pale he grew, and sat and trembled,
  While his eye the letter scanned ;
And his voice was choked and speechless,
  As he dropped it from his hand.

" Now what ails thee ? " cried Prince Yousuf.
  " Doth the king demand my head ? "
" Read it ! " gasps the good Alcayde.
  " Ah, my lord — would I were dead ! "

Yousuf read : " When this shall reach you,
  Slay my brother, and his head

Straightway by the bearer send me;
  So I may be sure he's dead."

"So" — cried Yousuf. " This I looked for.
  Now let us play out our game.
I was losing — you were winning
  When this ugly message came."

All confused. the poor Alcayde
  Played his knights and bishops wrong;
And the prince his moves corrected.
  So in silence sat they long.

In his mind Prince Yousuf pondered,
  " Why this hasty message send,
If my kind and thoughtful brother
  Were not hastening to his end?

" Surely he is ill or dying.
  And if I must lose my head,
My young nephew will succeed him
  O'er Grenada in my stead.

" Though my keeper still is friendly,
  I must gain some hours' delay.
He is poor : the king may bribe him.
  He may change ere close of day."

Then aloud — " Come, good Alcayde —
　　One more game before I die.
And be sure you make no blunders —
　　I may beat you yet.　I 'll try."

In his lonely life the keeper
　　Dearly loved his game of chess ;
Therefore needs he little urging,
　　Though sad thoughts his soul oppress.

For an hour or two they battled,
　　And the Alcayde gained amain ;
For the prince with restless glances
　　Gazed beyond the window-pane.

Still the chess-board lay between them ;
　　And the Alcayde played his best ;
Took no note of gliding hours,
　　Till the sunset fired the west.

Yet he gained not, for Prince Yousuf
　　With a sudden checkmate sprang
Unforeseen — and that same moment —
　　Hark — was that a bugle rang ?

Through the western windows gazing
　　Far across the dusty plain,

Yousuf saw the flash of lances —
   And the bugle rang again.

And two knights appeared advancing
   Like two eagles on the wing.
Allah Akbar!   From Grenada
   Faces flushed with joy they bring.
The king is dead!   Long live King Yousuf!
   Long lost lord — our rightful king!

ROSAMOND.

In the fragrant bright June morning, Rosamond, the
    queen of girls,
Down the marble doorsteps loiters, radiant with her
    sunny curls ;
O'er the green sward through the garden passes to the
    river's brink —
Throws away an old bouquet, and wonders if 't will float
    or sink.
Then returning through the garden, round and round the
    lawn she goes,
Singing, as she cuts fresh roses, she herself her world's
    fair rose ;
In her dainty morning-robe and straw hat shading half
    her face —
Picturesque in form and feature, lovely in her youth
    and grace ;
In her hand a little dagger, sharp and glittering in the
    sun,
Rifling hearts of thorny bushes, cutting roses one by one,
Pink and white and blood-red crimson — some in bud
    and some full-blown,

There through lawn and grove and garden sings she to
herself alone ;

Softly sings in broken snatches some old song of Spain
or France,

As she holds her roses off at full arm's length, with
sidelong glance,

Shifting groups of forms and colors ; for a painter's eye
hath she,

And all beauty pleaseth her, so artist-like and fancy-free.

Now she enters her boudoir and sets her roses in a vase.

There for seven days and nights their bloom and fragrance fill the place.

When the petals droop and fade, she 'll bear them to
the river's brink ;

Singing, throw them on the waves, and wonder if they 'll
float or sink.

Will she bear away to-night a bunch of lovers' rose-
hearts, pray ?

Set them in her vase a week — then throw them with
her flowers away ?

A QUESTION.

AH, who can tell which guide were best
    To truth long sought, but unattained —
The early faith, or late unrest?
    What age has earned, or boyhood gained?

When down life's vista as we gaze,
    Where vanished youth's remembered gleam,
The radiance of the unconscious days —
    The dream that knew not 't was a dream —

The time ere yet the shades of doubt
    Before our steps crept lengthening on,
And morn and noon spread all about
    Their warm and fragrant benison —

Was this a vision of the mind
    That comes but once and disappears?
And can our riper wisdom find
    A clearer path in after years?

The lore of philosophic age,
  The legendary creed of youth —
Say which should trace upon life's page
  The book-mark of the surest truth?

Ah, question not. The unconscious life
  That leaps to its spontaneous deed
Alone can harmonize the strife
  Between the impulse and the deed.

Through dark and light — through change on change
  The planet-soul is pledged to move,
Steeped all along its spinning range
  In sunshine born of thought and love.

MY STUDIO.

I LOVE it, yet I hardly can tell why —
My studio with its window to the sky,
Far up above the noises of the street,
The rumbling carts, the ceaseless tramp of feet;
A privacy secure from idle crowds,
And public only to the flying clouds.
No shadowed corners round about me hide.
Clear-lighted stand its walls on every side,
Each sketch and picture showing at its best.
A room for cheery work that needs no rest.
Only too short these days of autumn seem,
Where labor is but joy and peace supreme ;
Where fields and woods, towns, skies, and winding rills
Still haunt the memory as the canvas fills.
And while the painter plies his earnest task,
He seems as in some vision-land to bask ;
And all that fed his eye and fired his soul
When in the golden summer days he stole
Their forms and colors. now lived o'er again,
Runs like a strain of music through his brain.

O joyous tasks of art! without your spell
Life were a dull and dreary cloister-cell,
All nature darkened and all beauty dim.
But ye fill up its chalice to the brim
With draughts as sweet as ever yet, I ween,
Flowed in the poets' sparkling Hippocrene.

TALENT AND GENIUS.

I.

On the high road travelling steady,
Sure, alert, and ever ready,
Prompt to seize all fit occasion,
Courting power and wealth and station;
One clear aim before him keeping
With a vigilance unsleeping;
Prizing most the ephemeral flower
Blooming for a brilliant hour;
With self-conscious action moving;
Well known truths intent on proving;
Radiant in his day and season
With the world's reflected reason;
Noting times, effects, and causes,
Phaon wins the crowd's applauses.

II.

Wing'd like an eagle o'er mountains and meadows,
Lit by their splendors or hid by their shadows;
Borne by a power supernal, resistless;
Dreaming through trances abstracted and listless;

Swooping capricious to faults and to errors,
Redeemed by a virtue unconscious of terrors ;
Linking with ease his result and endeavor ;
Opening through chaos fresh pathways forever ;
Gilding the world with his thoughts and his fancies ;
Scornful of fashions and heedless of chances ;
Yet in obscurity living and dying —
Hylas, a voice in the wilderness crying,
Only is heard when no hand can restore him,
Only is known when the grave closes o'er him.

VENICE.

WHILE the skies of this northern November
    Scowl down with a darkening menace,
I wonder if you still remember
    That marvellous summer in Venice.

When the mornings by clouds unencumbered
    Smiled on in unchanging persistence
On the broad bright laguna that slumbered
    Afar in the magical distance.

And the mirror of waters reflected
    The sails in their gay plumage grouping
Like tropical birds that erected
    Their wings, or sat drowsily drooping.

How by moonlight our gondola gliding
    Through gleams and through shadows of wonder,
With its sharp flashing beak flew dividing
    The waves slipping silently under.

Then almost too full seemed the chalice
  Of new brimming life and of beauty,
As we floated by Riva and palace,
  Dogana and stately Salute —

Through deep-mouthed canals overshaded
  By balconies gray, quaint and olden,
Where ruins of centuries faded
  Stood stripped of their azure and golden.

Do you call back the days when before us
  The masters of art shone revealing
Their marvels of color — and o'er us
  Glowed grand on the rich massy ceiling

In the halls of the doges, where trembled
  The state in its turbulent fever,
And purple-robed senates assembled
  In days that are shadows forever?

You remember the yellow light tipping
  The domes when the sunset was dying;
The crowds on the quays, and the shipping;
  The pennons and flags that were flying; —

Saint Mark's with its mellow-toned glory,
  The splendor and gloom of its riches;

The columns Byzantine and hoary;
   The arches, the gold-crusted niches;

And the days when the sunshine invited
   The painters abroad, until mooring
Their bark in the shadow, delighted
   They wrought at their labors alluring;

The pictures receding in stretches
   Of amber and opal around us —
The joy of our mornings of sketches —
   The spell of achievement that bound us?

Ah, never I busy my brushes
   With scenes of that radiant weather,
But through me the memory rushes
   When we were in Venice together.

Fair Venice, the pearl-shell of cities!
   Though poor the oblations we bring her —
The pictures, the songs and the ditties —
   Ah, still we must paint her and sing her!

A vision of beauty long vanished,
   A dream that is joy to remember,
A solace that cannot be banished
   By all the chill blasts of November!

THE TWO DREAMS.

I MET one in the Land of Sleep
 Who seemed a friend long known and true.
I woke. That friend I could not keep —
 For him I never knew.

Yet there was one in life's young morn
 Loved me, I thought, as I loved him.
Slow from that trance I waked forlorn,
 To find his love grown dim.

He by whose side in dreams I ranged,
 Unknown by name, my friend still seems;
While he I knew so well has changed.
 So both were only dreams.

AT THE GRAVE OF KEATS.

TO G. W. C.

LONG, long ago, in the sweet Roman spring
    Through the bright morning air we slowly strolled,
And in the blue heaven heard the skylarks sing
    Above the ruins old —

Beyond the Forum's crumbling grass-grown piles,
    Through high-walled lanes o'erhung with blossoms
        white
That opened on the far Campagna's miles
    Of verdure and of light ;

Till by the grave of Keats we stood, and found
    A rose some loyal hand had planted there.
Making more sacred still that hallowed ground,
    And that enchanted air.

A single rose, whose fading petals drooped,
    And seemed to wait for us to gather them.
So, kneeling on the humble mound, we stooped
    And plucked it from its stem.

One rose, and nothing more.   We shared its leaves
　Between us, as we shared the thoughts of one
Called from the fields before his unripe sheaves
　Could feel the harvest sun.

That rose's fragrance is forever fled
　For us, dear friend — but not the poet's lay.
He is the rose — deathless among the dead —
　Whose perfume lives to-day.

BROKEN WINGS.

GRAY-HEADED POETS, whom the full years bless
  With life and health and chance still multiplied
To hold your forward course — fame and success
  Close at your side;

Who easier won your bays because the fields
  Lacked reapers; — time has been your helper long.
Rich are the crops your busy tillage yields —
  Your arms still strong.

Honor to you, your talent and your truth.
  As ye have soared and sung, still may ye sing!
Yet we remember some who fell in youth
  With broken wing.

Names nigh forgotten now, by time erased,
  Or else placarded o'er by those long known,
Had fate permitted, might they not have blazed
  Beside your own?

Ah yes, due fame for all who have achieved;
  And yet a thought for those who died too young —

Their green fruit dropped — their visions half con-
    ceived —
  Their lays unsung!

A tribute song for them!   Reach forth, renowned
  And honored ones, from your green sunny glades,
And grasp their spirit-hands — the bards uncrowned
  Amid the shades.

Not those whom glory follows to a bier
  Enshrined in marble, decked with costly flowers.
The loud world speaks their praise from year to-year.
  They need not ours.

But for the dead whose promise failed through death,
  The great who might have been — whose early bloom
Dropping like roses in the north-wind's breath,
  Found but a tomb.

Yet it may be. in some bright land, unchecked
  By fate — some fair Elysian field unknown,
Their brows by brighter laurel wreaths are decked —
  Their seat a throne ;

While spirits of the illustrious dead. the seers,
  Prophets and poets of the olden days
Mingle, perchance, with theirs, as with their peers,
  Immortal lays.

SEA PICTURES.

I.

MORNING.

THE morning sun has pierced the mist,
And beach and cliff and ocean kissed.
Blue as the lapis-lazuli
The sea reflects the azure sky.
In the salt healthy breeze I stand
Upon the solid floor of sand.
Along the untrodden shore are seen
Fresh tufts of weed maroon and green,
And ruffled kelp and stranded sticks
And shells and stones and sea-moss mix.
The low black rocks, forever wet,
Lie tangled in their pulpy net.
The shy sand-pipers fly and light —
And swallows circle out of sight.
Out where the sky the horizon meets
Glide glimmering sails in scattered fleets.
Old Ocean smiles as though amid
His leagues of brine no treachery hid.
And safe upon the sandy marge,
By stranded boat and floating barge,

Gay children leap and laugh and run,
Browned by the salt air and the sun.

II.

EVENING.

Now thickening twilight presses **down**
Upon the harbor and the town,
And all around a misty pall
Of dull gray cloud hangs over all.
The huddling fishing-sloops lie safe,
While far away the breakers chafe.
And now the landsman's straining eye
Mingles the gray sea with the sky.
Far out upon the darkening deep
The white ghosts of the ocean leap.
Boone Island's light, a lonely star,
Is flashing o'er the waves afar.
Up the broad beach the sea rolls in
In never-ending foam and din ;
And all along the craggy shore
Resounds one long continuous roar.
We turn away, and hail each gleam
Where lamps from cottage windows **stream.**
For sad and solemn is the moan
Of ocean when the day has flown,
And, borne on dusky wings, the night
Wraps in a shroud the dying light.

ARS LONGA, VITA BREVIS.

I STARTED on a lonely road.
 A few companions with me went.
Some fell behind, some forward strode,
 But all on one high purpose bent :

To live for Nature, finding truth
 In beauty, and the shrines of art;
To consecrate our joyous youth
 To aims outside the common mart.

The way was steep, though pleasure crowned
 Our toil with every step we took.
The morning air was spiced around
 From many a pine and cedar nook.

I turned aside and lingered long
 To pluck a rose, to hear a bird,
To muse, while listening to the song
 Of brooks through leafy coverts heard ;

To live in thoughts that brought no fame
 Or guerdon from the thoughtless crowd ;

To toil for ends that could not claim
 The world's applauses coarse and loud;

Then onward pressed. But far before
 I saw my comrades on the heights.
They no divided homage bore
 To Beauty's myriad sounds and sights.

In blithe self-confidence they wrought.
 Some strove for fame and fame's reward.
They pleased the public's facile thought;
 Then paused and stretched them on the sward.

And still though oft I bind my sheaf
 In fields my comrades have not known;
Though Art is long and life is brief,
 And youth has now forever flown,

I would not lose the raptures sweet,
 Nor scorn the toil of earlier years;
Still would I climb with eager feet,
 Though towering height on height appears —

And up the mountain road I see
 A younger throng with voices loud,
Who side by side press on with me,
 Till I am lost amid the crowd.

LOVE'S VOYAGE.

As once I sat upon the shore
   There came to me a fairy boat,
A bark I never saw before,
   Whose coming I had failed to note,
Wrapped in my studies conning rules of life by rote.

The stern was fashioned like a heart;
   The curving sides like Cupid's bow.
And from the mast, which like a dart
   Was winged above and barbed below,
A pennon like an airy stream of blood did flow.

Upon the prow on either side
   Was carved a snowy Paphian dove.
Between, reflected in the tide
   An arching swan's neck rose above
The deck o'erspread with broidered tapestries of love.

Against the mast the idle sail
   Flapped like a lace-edged valentine.
It seemed a canvas all too frail,

Should winds arouse the sleeping brine.
A toy the boat appeared, for sport in weather fine.

And so I stepped, in idle mood,
  Aboard the bark — when suddenly
A breeze sprang up : and while I stood
  Uncertain, thinking I was free
To make retreat, the vessel bore me out to sea.

Silent and swift away from land
  It cut the waves.   No pilot steered.
No voice of captain gave command.
  Yet to and fro it tacked and veered.
All day it flew.   At eve a distant land appeared.

An island in the restless seas,
  With rosy cliffs, and gold and green
Of dappled fields, and tropic trees,
  With trailing vines and flowers between,
Across the purple waves through amber skies was seen.

And music floating from afar
  I heard, of voice and instrument
As the sun sank, and star by star
  Throbbed in the living firmament ;
And all kind fates seemed pledged to cheer me as I
    went.

Till in a deep and shadowy bay
 The little argosy, self-furled,
Self-anchored, in the silence lay,
 And landed me upon a world
By other stars and moons endiamonded, impearled.

A region to my student's nooks
 Unknown — where first I learned to see
That love is never conned from books,
 Nor passion taught by fantasy —
But in the living, beating heart alone can be.

For on that shore a maiden stood,
 Who smiled with sympathetic glance,
And when I pressed her hand, and wooed,
 Turned not her truthful eyes askance,
And proved my voyage was no idle sport of chance.

Ah, from this island if I veer
 Into the seas of worldly strife,
Give me the bark that brought me here,
 Where now the tried and faithful wife
Year after year renews the lover's lease of life.

SURVIVAL OF THE FITTEST.

"Naught but the fittest lives," I hear
    Ring on the northern breeze of thought:
"To Nature's heart the strong are dear,
    The weak must pass unloved, unsought."

And yet in undertones a voice
    Is heard that says, "O child of earth,
Your mind's best work, your heart's best choice
    Shall stand with God for what they are worth."

Time's buildings are not all of stone.
    With frailest fibres Nature spins
Her living webs from zone to zone,
    And what is lost she daily wins.

I fain would think, amid the strife
    Between realities and forms.
Slight gifts may claim perennial life
    'Mid slow decay and sudden storms.

This tuft of silver hairs I loose
    From open windows to the breeze.

Some bird of spring perchance may use
  To build her nest in yonder trees.

These pictures painted with an art
  Surpassed by younger sight and skill,
May pass into some friendly heart,
  Some room with Nature's smiles may fill.

These leaves of light and earnest rhyme
  Dropped on the windy world, though long
Neglected now, some future time
  May weave into its nest of song.

A WORD TO PHILOSOPHERS.

Cold philosophers, so apt
  With your formulas exacting,
In your problems so enwrapt,
  And your theories distracting;

Webs of metaphysic doubt
  On your wheels forever spinning,
Turning Nature inside out
  From its end to its beginning;

Drawing forth from matter raw
  Protoplasmic threads, to fashion
What Creation never saw —
  Mind apart from faith or passion;

Faculties that know no wants
  But a logical position —
Intellectual cormorants
  Fed on facts of pure cognition; —

Like Arachne's is your task,
  By Minerva's wisdom baffled.

Defter weavers we must ask ;
   Tissues less obscurely ravelled.

Larger vision you must find
   Ere your evolution-plummets
Sound the abysses of the mind,
   Or your measure reach its summits.

Not from matter crude and coarse
   Comes this delicate creation.
Twinned with it a finer force
   Rules it to its destination.

All beliefs, affections, deeds
   Feed its depths as streams a river,
Every purpose holds the seeds
   Of a fruit that grows forever.

Souls outsoar your schoolmen's wit,
   In a loftier heaven wheeling.
Lights ideal o'er them flit.
   Every thought is wing'd with feeling.

Conscience born of heavenly light
   Mingles with their lofty yearning ;
Phantasy and humor bright
   Cheer their toilsome path of learning.

Poesy with dreamy eyes
  Lures them into fairy splendor,
Music's magic harmonies
  Thrill with touches deep and tender.

Love, that shapes their mental moods,
  Offers now its warm oblations,
Now the heart's dark solitudes
  Glow with solemn adorations.

Vain your biologic strife,
  Your asserting, your denying ;
Ygdrasil the Tree of Life
  Flouts your narrow classifying.

Every living leaf and bud
  On its mighty branches growing,
Palpitates with will and blood
  Past primordial foreknowing.

Your dissecting-knives can show
  Less than half these wondrous natures,
In these beating hearts there glow
  Flames that scorch your nomenclatures, —

Lights that make your axioms fine
  Fade like stars when day is breaking ; —
Splendors, hopes, and powers divine,
  New born with each day's awaking.

Raise your scientific lore,
    Grant us larger definitions ;
Souls are surely something more
    Than mere bundles of cognitions.

Take the sum — the mighty whole —
    Man, this sovereign Protean creature,
Follow the all-embracing soul,
    If you can, through form and feature.

Whence it came in vain you guess,
    Where it goes you cannot measure,
And its depths are fathomless ;
    And exhaustless flows its treasure.

And its essence holds the world
    In abeyance and solution,
For the gods themselves are furled
    In its mystic involution.

THE COAL-FIRE.

1.

COME. we 'll light the parlor fire ;
  Winter sets in sharp and rough.
Wood is dear, but coal 's provided,
  For three months, I think, enough.
Bring one hod of Lackawanna,
  One of Sidney's softer kind,
Mix them well — clap on the blower,
  Let the grate outroar the wind.

2.

See — they are coming — the guests I expected,
  Not a man's party, o'er punch and cigars ;
Sexes must blend in the friends I've selected,
  Moonlight must mellow the glittering stars.
Soon will it kindle, the blithe conversation,
  Spirits to spirits responsively fit ;
Men with their logic and grave moderation,
  Women with sentiment, gossip and wit.

3.

Now the softly flaming Sidney
  Mixes with the anthracite ;

Quickens all its slow-paced ardor
  With a fluttering glow and light;
While their heat and radiance blended
  Flash in gleams of red and blue,
Filling all the room with sunshine,
  Gaily sparkling up the flue.

4.

Lonely was Adam till Eve came to cheer him —
  Came to commingle her warmth with his light.
Man is a fossil till woman comes near him,
  A rose on his brier — a moon to his night.
Then when the tenderer feminine color
  Rims the hard stalk with its delicate gleams,
All his best life growing sweeter and fuller
  Wakes in the glow of those holier beams.

5.

Hard and soft in cordial union
  Now have fused, like molten wax.
Each a temper gives and borrows —
  Each the half the other lacks.
Should they lose their flames and smoulder
  With a dull and sullen light,
Stir them up — the sparking Sidney
  Soon will start the anthracite.

6.

What — have my guests then exhausted their topics?
Why is this lull in the murmur of tongues?
Where is that breath from the flowery tropics?
Lead to the piano our empress of songs!
Music shall stir us to harmonies hidden,
Flooding to rapture like beakers of wine.
Stories shall move us to laughter unbidden;
Laughter like music is something divine.

7.

Ah, 't is midnight!   Are you going?
Parties will break up so soon.
Count not hours so swiftly flowing,
Heed not the high wintry moon.
One more song before we sever,
And the cinders turn to white:
One old story, good as ever!
No?   Too late?   Ah, well — good night!

8.

Now they have gone with the pale dying embers.
Here in my parlor, still cosy and warm
With the glow of the hearth, how my fancy remem-
bers
Each guest of the evening — each talent and
charm; —

The slow-burning fervors of masculine reason,
　The swift-glancing flame of the feminine heart ; —
And I vow that no fire shall be lit at this season,
　But coal of each sex shall contribute its part.

TWO VIEWS OF IT.

BEFORE the daybreak, in the murky night
My chanticleer, half dreaming, sees the light
Stream from my window on his perch below,
And taking it for dawn he needs must crow.

Wakeful and sad I shut my book, and smile
To think my lonely vigil should beguile
The silly fowl.   Alas, I find no ray
Within my lamp or heart, of dawning day.

OLD AND YOUNG.

1.

THEY soon grow old who grope for gold
In marts where all is bought and sold ;
Who live for self, and on some shelf
In darkened vaults hoard up their pelf
Cankered and crusted o'er with mould.
For them their youth itself is old.

2.

They ne'er grow old who gather gold
Where spring awakes and flowers unfold;
Where suns arise in joyous skies,
And fill the soul within their eyes.
For them the immortal bards have sung,
For them old age itself is young.

THE VICTORIES OF PEACE.

1.

GONE is the tempest that clouded
  The land with its dark desolation.
Out from the pall that enshrouded
  Leaps the new strength of the nation.

2.

Never again shall the cannon
  Roar with their terrible voicing,
Save where the free flag and pennon
  Wave o'er a country rejoicing.

3.

Boast not when musketry rattles
  O'er corpses of landsmen and seamen.
Gains that are greater than battles
  Come with the ballots of freemen.

4.

Praise ye the peace that engenders
  Trust in a people enlightened ;
Honor to valiant defenders,
  Hope for the days that have brightened.

SUMMER DAWN.

SOME summer mornings — when you've taken tea
Too late the night before — perhaps you'll see,
If at some Berkshire farmhouse far away
You chance to wake while yet the sky is gray,
A glory, to your landscape-painter men
Unknown, yet worthy of a poet's pen.

Look from your window.   Long gray banks of cloud
The fields, the hills, the distant view enshroud.
Faint stars still glimmer in the heavens above.
Below dim shapes of fog o'er stream and grove
Hang wreathing, shifting in the sluggish breeze.
Are yonder shadows mist, or mist-clad trees?
For what is cloud and what is land no eye
(Sleepy at least like yours) can yet descry.
And now the rushing streams, by day unheard,
You hear, and now the twitter of a bird,
And now another, till at last the hills
And woods are all alive with fugues and trills.
The sheep begin to bleat, the cows to low;
Three hoarse, young roosters try their best to crow,

Responding to some thirsty, quacking duck,
Or hen who folds her chicks with motherly cluck.

Now morning spreads apace.   The stars are drowned.
Trees loom above the fog ; and all around
The landscape is transfigured in the light
Of pearly skies.   Westward the wings of Night
Are folded as she steals unseen away.
Now in the far northeast an amber gray
Gleams under bars of long dark-pencilled cloud.
The crows above the woods are cawing loud.
Brighter and brighter up the dewy slope
The coming sunrise floods the lands with hope.
The clouds from north to south begin to blush.
Old Graylock answers with a rosy flush.
One mountain peak looms up with crimsoned sides ;
A moment more, and in the mist it hides.
And now the valleys catch the sun below,
And elms and barn-roofs redden in the glow.

O for a pencil rapid as the light
To paint the glories bursting on the sight !
Making the plain New England landscape seem
The unfamiliar scenery of a dream.
For this might be in Arcady — my rhyme
Some Eastern shepherd's of the olden time.
Here might I pipe with Tityrus in the grove ;
Here to fair Amaryllis whisper love ;

Here the wild woodland haunts of Dryads seek —
But what is that! The locomotive's shriek
Calls me from Dreamland and the Arcadian dawn.
The sun is up. The mystery is gone.
Another book of poesy the West
Has opened. Let the bards of old go rest.

THE OLD APPLE-WOMAN.

A BROADWAY LYRIC.

SHE sits by the side of a turbulent stream
  That rushes and rolls forever
Up and down like a weary dream
  In the trance of a burning fever.

Up and down through the long Broadway
  It flows with its tiresome paces —
Down and up through the noisy day,
  A river of feet and of faces.

Seldom a drop of that river's spray
  Touches her withered features ;
Yet still she sits there day by day
  In the throng of her fellow-creatures.

Apples and cakes and candy to sell,
  Daily before her lying.
The ragged newsboys know her well —
  The rich never think of buying.

Year in, year out, in her dingy shawl
   The wind and the rain she weathers,
Patient and mute at her little stall ;
   But few are the coppers she gathers.

Still eddies the crowd intent on gain.
   Each for himself is striving
With selfish heart and seething brain —
   An endless hurry and driving.

The loud carts rattle in thunder and dust ;
   Gay Fashion sweeps by in its coaches.
With a vacant stare she mumbles her crust,
   She is past complaints and reproaches.

Still new faces and still new feet —
   The same yet changing forever ;
They jostle along through the weary street,
   The waves of the human river.

Withered and dry like a leafless bush
   That clings to the bank of a torrent,
Year in, year out, in the whirl and the rush,
   She sits, of the city's current.

The shrubs of the garden will blossom again
   Though far from the flowing river ;
But the spring returns to her in vain —
   Its bloom has nothing to give her.

Yet in her heart there buds the hope
  Of a Father's love and pity;
For her the clouded skies shall ope,
  And the gates of a heavenly city.

THE WEATHER-PROPHET.

A FABLE.

"What can the matter be with the thermometer?
Is it the sun or the moon or the comet, or
Something broke loose in the old earth's pedometer?"
Thus in his study a weather philosopher
Mused — every minute more puzzled and cross over.
Wind-charts and notes he proceeded to toss over.
"Up in this tower, this breezy and barren height,
One should be cool as an elderly Sharonite.
Something is wrong with the scales of my Fahrenheit.
'T was but this morning the wind blowing northerly
Roughened the tops of the ocean waves frothily ;
Now it has shifted, and seems to be southerly " —
(These are not rhymes — I am fully aware of it.
But the hot weather — for he had the care of it —
Fully excused him, and I have no share of it.)

Time to this sage was so precious that never he
Ate at regular hour ; forever he
Seemed to be lost in a weather-wise reverie.

So a small kitchen the town-folks did make for him
Right underneath, where a servant could bake for him,
Boil for him, cook up a chop or a steak for him,
So that he need n't be starving while measuring
Rain-storms and calms that the heavens were treasuring.
'T was a bright thought which they took a great pleas-
    ure in ;
For 't was the weather that made the great theme for
    them.
This was their day-talk and this their night's dream for
    them.
Here was the man who could skim the sky's cream for
    them ;
Thousands of miles away see a cloud-macula —
Tell what was coming in language oracular —
Translate his science in common vernacular.
Quite independent of housekeeping syndicates
He could pronounce what the weather-glass indicates
Long ere old Boreas had opened his windy gates.
Knew all the signs from the Crab to Aquarius,
Shifting or permanent — single or various ;
Bright signs that gladden us, dark signs that weary us,
Versed in the trade-winds and currents could spy a way
How a storm-centre in Texas or Iowa
Might prove a cyclone or peaceably die away.
Skilled in all secrets of meteorology,
Clear in his mind as that H I should follow G.
If he made blunders he made no apology.

He was the boldest of Old Probabilities ;
Scorned all assistance and short-hand facilities.
Ah, what a thing to have genius and skill it is !
Pity if he should be forced to take off his eye ;
Leave for a dinner his notes to a novice eye !
Food was a trifle for one who could prophesy.
So like the prophet of old when the city he
Left for the woods, and the ravens had pity, he
Found himself served by a black-coat committee.

Now while engrossed in his figures, not dreaming it,
Bridget below in the kitchen was steaming it ;
Making the building so hot that ice-cream in it
Melted like butter.   Her stove and the range in it
Cooking his dinner — though this may seem strange
        in it —
Was the sole reason the air had a change in it.
Over his figures his brow getting rigid, he
Kept at his task, never thinking of Bridgety —
Growing each minute more fussy and fidgety.
Up through the speaking-tube rushed the hot air on him,
Bringing the steam of the boiler to bear on him.
So with a mystified sort of despair on him
Soon he proceeded to write and to scratch away,
And by his telegraph sent a despatch away —
(Never before was Old Prob so *infatué*)
Saying — " It seems by my Aëroscopical
Great heats with thunder will soon be the topic all —

Weather, in short, most decidedly tropical.
Can it be sun-spots? Volcanic impurities
Caused by a meteor bursting? I'm sure it is
Something abnormal — but very obscure it is!
Possibly something may ail my thermometer;
Possibly 't is the effect of the comet, or
Something broke loose in the old Earth's pedometer."

MORAL.

Prophets are struck now and then with insanity.
Ever since Adam man's measureless vanity
Thinks his own mood is the mind of humanity.

OMAR KHAYYÁM.

READING in Omar till the thoughts that burned
Upon his pages seemed to be inurned
    Within me in a silent fire, my pen
By instinct to his flowing metre turned.

Vine-crowned free-thinker of thy Persian clime —
Brave bard whose daring thought and mystic rhyme
    Through English filter trickles down to us
Out of the lost springs of an olden time —

Baffled by life's enigmas, like the crowd
Who strove before and since to see the cloud
    Lift from the mountain pinnacles of faith —
We honor still the doubts thou hast avowed,

And fain would round the half-truth of thy dream;
And fain let in — if so we might — a beam
    Of purer light through windows of the soul,
Dividing things that are from things that seem.

True, true, brave poet, in thy cloud involved,
The riddle of the world stood all unsolved ;
    And we who boast our broader views still grope
Too oft like thee, though centuries have revolved.

Yet this we know. Thy symbol of the jar
Suits not our western manhood, left to mar
    Or make, in part, the clay 't is moulded of:
And the soul's freedom is its fateful star.

Not like thy ball thrown from the player's hand
Inert and passive on a yielding strand ;
    Or if a ball, the rock whence it rebounds
Proves that e'en this some license may command.

But though thy mind, which measured Jove and Mars,
Lay fettered from the Unseen by bolts and bars
    Of circumstance, one truth thy spirit saw,
The mystery spanning life and earth and stars.

Dervish and threatening dogma were thy foes.
The question though unanswered still arose;
    And through the revel and the wine-cups still
The honest thought, " Who knows, but One — who
      knows ? "

And as I read again each fervent line
That smiles through sighs, and drips with fragrant wine ;

And Vedder's thoughtful muse has graced the verse
With added jewels from the artist's mine —

I read a larger meaning in the sage,
A modern comment on a far-off age ;
  And take the truth, and leave the error out
That casts its light stain on the Asian page.

LONGFELLOW.

Across the sea the swift sad message darts
And beats with sudden pang against our hearts.
Under the elm-trees in his homestead old
The Laureate of our land lies dead and cold;
Wept by the love of friends, and crowned with **fame**;
Revered by youth and age, his well-known name
Caught in fast-circling whispers, sad and low,
In streets where noisy crowds move too and fro —
" Can it be true that he is dead — is dead ? "
Life seemed to love that noble, silvery head,
And youth still lingered in the kindly eyes
Now closed, alas, to all beneath the skies !

No more across the fields by Charles's stream
Those eyes shall see their well-loved landscape **gleam**.
No more the treasured books upon his shelves
Suggest the visions rarer than themselves.
No friends around his hospitable fire
Hear the last touches of his graceful lyre.

The coming spring will flush with purple bloom
His lilacs, and waft in their sweet perfume;

His roses unregarded drop away ;
Unheard the oriole's warble through the day ;
Unmarked the bees' low hum from flower to flower,
The dial's shade, the sunshine and the shower.
Yet from the garden of his thoughts and deeds
Still will his poems fly like winged seeds.
And far and wide, through city, plain and hill,
Borne to a thousand firesides, bloom and fill
The people's hearts, and touch to issues fine
Of aspiration human and divine.

PARIS, *March* 28, 1882.

RALPH WALDO EMERSON.

Out of the cloud that dimmed his sunset light,
  Into the unknown firmament withdrawn
Beyond the mists and shadows of the night,
  We mourn the friend and teacher who has gone.

As in the days of old when Plato freed
  The Athenian youths into a heavenlier sphere,
Long will the age with reverence hear and heed
  The sweet deep music of our poet-seer.

For to his eye all objects and events
  Spoke a symbolic language ; and his mind
Pierced with the poet's vision through the dense
  Dull surface to the larger truth behind.

And yet no solitary mystic trained
  To spin a metaphysic web was he ;
But open-eyed to all that life contained,
  And the broad earth, of living harmony.

Nature adopted him from boyhood's hour.
  The pines, the elms, the willows knew him well.

The lonely streams where blushed the cardinal-flower,
  And where the shy Rhodora's petals fell.

And well his mother's lore he loved and learned;
  His master-hand her crudest stuff refined.
All that she gave he back to her returned
  Woven with figures of the shaping mind.

It seemed as if the hill-tops where he met
  The sunrise still the livery put on
Of nobler days, and never could forget
  The Syrian splendors of the poet's dawn.

And books to him unfolded all their store;
  What soul was in them he had eyes to see.
And past and present turned up golden ore,
  Transmuted by his mind's fine alchemy.

He drew his circles of so wide a sweep
  That they encompassed every sect and creed.
Beneath the thought which seemed to others deep
  His swifter spirit dived with brilliant speed.

His keen, clear intuition knit the threads
  Of truths disjoined in one symmetric whole;
And barren wayside weeds and scattered shreds
  Of facts found mystic meanings in his soul.

He dared to ope the windows to the breeze
　Of Nature, when sectarians shuddering frowned,
While through the close air of their cloistered ease
　The leaves of creeds fell fluttering to the ground;

Yet lived to see harsh theologians change
　From blind mistrust to love the truth he taught;
And shallow wits grow dumb beneath his range
　Of brilliant apothegm and daring thought.

Choice words and images like Shakspeare's best
　Dropped from his lips and waited on his pen.
His voice in tuneful eloquence expressed
　The manliest minds of Plutarch's noblest men.

For him our Western world its keen, dry lore
　Recorded with a stenographic hand,
While the far Orient climes for tribute bore
　The scriptures old of many a pagan land.

He saw the Soul whose breath all being breathes; —
　The Life that glows in atoms and in suns;
The Law that binds; the Beauty that enwreathes;
　The Ideal that all mortal wit outruns.

Yet close to earth and common duties bound,
　Pledged to all true and gracious tasks he stood.
His presence made a sunshine all around,
　His daily life a bond of brotherhood.

He needed not to worship at a shrine
   Purer than private hours might well approve.
His missal was illumed with thoughts divine,
   His rosary strung with kindly deeds of love.

Yet love and justice were at one with him;
   And on the base oppressor's brow the stain
And brand were laid, not in derision grim,
   But sad and fateful as the mark of Cain.

Thus, true as needle to the polar star,
   He espoused the righteous cause, rebuked the wrong,
And flashed chivalric 'gainst a nation's bar
   Of precedent, though fixed and sanctioned long.

Poet and sage! thy lofty muse demands
   An insight deeper than the times attain.
Across the stagnant pools and drifting sands
   Of thought I see thee like a sacred fane

Rise sunlit in the broad expanse of time;
   And young and old shall greet from far thy light,
And pilgrims turn from many an old-world clime
   To hail thy star-like dome of stainless white.

The wise will know thee, and the good will love.
   The age to come will feel thy impress given
In all that lifts the race a step above
   Itself, and stamps it with the seal of heaven.

FREDERICK HENRY HEDGE, D.D.

ON HIS 80TH BIRTHDAY, DEC. 12, 1885.

WHAT lapse or accident of time
Can dull that soul's sonorous chime
Which owns the priceless heritage —
Youth's summer warmth in wintry age ?
The gods can grant no rarer boon
Than heart with mind in genial tune,
Through a long life's vicissitudes
Unjarred by chances and by moods ;
A soul elastic and unworn
Whose eve retains the smile of morn ;
And all the poesy of youth
Is wedded to the soul of truth.

So have I seen the Alpine glow
On hoary pinnacles of snow,
While many a younger wilderness
Of woods beneath lay colorless
And darkling in the twilight sky,
Touched by no sunset alchemy.

For some there are whose youth is old
Long ere their youthful blood grows cold ;
And some in age so young that time,
Deceived, still sees them in their prime.

No form or face that prophesied
A strength to after years denied —
No spirit lost in aims that seem
The cloud-land of a worldly dream —
No head discrowned — no incomplete
And slackened course to-day we greet
In him whose fourscore years have spanned
The gulfs of fact and wonder-land ; —
Who brought the seeds of Europe's lore
To fertilize our western shore ; —
By pastoral care, by voice and pen
Toiling to serve his fellow-men ;
Who early stood in freedom's van,
And with forecasting eye outran
The cloudy creeds that long obscured
The light to later days assured.

What claim of youth by word or deed
Can e'er dislodge or supersede
The royal right to place and fame
Earned by long years of earnest aim,
Of learning deep, of vision wide,
Of wisdom to fit speech allied ;

While all along their downward trend
Youth's earlier lights his steps attend?
Still in the gloaming of his day
Lingers the glow that mocks decay.

Friend, poet, scholar, teacher, sage!
Unshadowed by the mists of age,
Long may the generous faith and thought,
The lights from the ideal caught,
That guided and inspired his youth,
Shine clearer toward the perfect truth.
And like some minster tower whose grand
Melodious bells ring o'er the land,
His voice be heard when daylight fails
Across the darkened hills and vales;
And ere night's pall be o'er him cast,
His mellowest music be his last.

SO FAR, SO NEAR.

Thou, so far, we grope to grasp thee —
Thou, so near, we cannot clasp thee —
Thou, so wise, our prayers grow heedless —
Thou, so loving, they are needless !
In each human soul thou shinest.
Human-best is thy divinest.
In each deed of love thou warmest;
Evil into good transformest.
Soul of all, and moving centre
Of each moment's life we enter.
Breath of breathing — light of gladness —
Infinite antidote of sadness ; —
All-preserving ether flowing
Through the worlds, yet past our knowing.
Never past our trust and loving,
Nor from thine our life removing.
Still creating, still inspiring,
Never of thy creatures tiring.
Artist of thy solar spaces,
And thy humble human faces;
Mighty glooms and splendors voicing;

In thy plastic work rejoicing;
Through benignant law connecting
Best with best — and all perfecting,
Though all human races claim thee,
Thought and language fail to name thee,
Mortal lips be dumb before thee,
Silence only may adore thee!

SONNETS.

I.

1.

THE Summer goes, with all its birds and flowers ;
The Autumn passes with its solemn sky ;
The Winter comes again — yet you and I
Know not the old companionship once ours.
The twilight mist between us hangs and lowers ;
Your face I see not — voice I cannot hear.
No letter tells me you in thought are near.
The west-wind blows and sweeps away the showers,
But from the west no whisper comes of you.
Friends press around you in your distant home —
(Your distant home I never yet have seen,)
And old familiar greetings still renew ;
While I with fancy's eyes alone can come
And peep unnoted there behind your screen.

II.

2.

PARTED by time and space for many a year,
Yet ever longing, hoping for a day
When, heart to heart, the happy weeks shall stay
Their flight for us, and all our sky be clear
As in our boyhood's spring — my brother dear,
You and I bide our time.   The buds of May
Shall blossom yet for us.   What though the gray
Of dusky Autumn eventide be near,
And silver locks and beards have changed us so
From what we were — you still to me are young,
And I to you.   The fireside of our loves
Shall be our summer, bright as in the glow
Of youth, when we, two blithe Arcadians, sung
And fluted in those old Virginia groves.

III.

3.

Ah, happy time ! when music bound in one
Two kindred souls that ne'er were out of tune :
When in the porch, beneath the summer moon,
Our supper o'er, our school-boy lessons done,
While other lads were at some boisterous fun,
We trilled our Tara's Hall or Bonnie Doon :
Or in some fire-lit wintry afternoon,
Our flutes, you first, I second, bravely won
Their winding path through many a tough duet;
Nor cared for plaudits louder than the praise
Mother or sisters, in those simple days,
Well pleased, bestowed : ah, sweeter than we met
In after-life, from critics pledged to raise
Art's standard high as dome or minaret.

IV.

4.

Friend, dear as Memory's joys! of life that's past
A part, and part of better life to come,
If life to come there be, in some dear home
Beyond the rigid clouds that overcast
Our sundered lives — all that is mine thou hast; —
All thoughts, all sympathies ; —though far I roam
From you — by mountains, streams, or ocean's foam
Divided long — yet ever, first and last,
Our love knows no division.   In my soul
And yours, we twin-born spirits of one blood,
Still, as of old, are one.   No sea can roll
Between its league-long melancholy flood,
No separate interests, loves, or pressing cares
Disturb the mutual trust our being shares.

V.

5.

ALL loves have frailer roots than loves that start
From one ancestral blood.   The friends we find
In youth pass on before us, or behind
Are dropped, or on diverging paths depart,
While branches from one trunk still own one heart,
And bud and bear from one maternal mind.
Sister and brother need no vows to bind
Their pre-ordained alliance, nor the art
Of lovers plotting through a thousand fears
Lest love, of passion born, should fade or change ;
Nor dread the undermining drip of years;
Nor stand on forms that other souls estrange.
Such love is ours, and theirs who bear our name,
Born in the honored home from which we came.

VI.

6.

Ah, many a time our memory slips aside
And leaves the round of present cares and joys,
To live again the time when we were boys;
To call our parents back with love and pride;
To see again the dear ones who have died;
To dream once more amid the household toys,
The sports, the jests, the masquerades, the noise,
The blaze and sparkle of the wood fireside;
The books, the drawings, and the merry press
Around the blithe tea-board; the evenings long;
Rattling backgammon and still, solemn chess;
And best of all when instrument and song
Bore us to visionary lands and streams,
And crowned our nights with coronals of dreams.

VII.

7.

THOSE times are gone, that circle thinned away,
And we who live, now scattered far and wide,
Each in our separate centres fixed abide,
Round which new interests now revolve and play
In separate loves and duties day by day.
Yet, by the records of old loves allied,
We clasp each other's hands beneath the tide
Of time, and cling together as we may.
Even so beneath the sea the throbbing wires
That bind the sundered continents in one,
In space-annihilating pulses thrill
With swift-winged words and purpose and desires.
Our earlier visions haunt our memories still,
And age grows young in friendship's quickening sun.

VIII.

8.

You were not born to hide such gifts as yours
'Neath dreary law-books, nor amid the dust
And dry routine of desks to sit and rust
Where clerks plod through their tasks on office-floors.
Let duller laborers drudge through daily chores,
And do what fate for them makes fit and just.
You bravely do your work because you must;
And when released, your genius sings and soars.
Such humor from your pen hath ever run
In pictures or in letters all unforced,
As Hogarth, Lamb, or Dickens might have done;
Finer than many a noted wit, who, horsed
Upon the people's favor, waves his blade
Like Harlequin, and makes his jests his trade.

IX.

9.

I NEEDS must praise the natural gifts of one
Who praises not himself, nor seeks for praise ;
Too unambitious for these emulous days,
When each small talent seeks the public sun,
And victors' wreaths are worn before they are won.
So true to conscience that he oft betrays
Himself, o'ervaluing standards others raise,
Or underrating what himself has done.
Who might have risen in letters or in art ;
But faithful to the work he early chose,
To that he gave his time, if not his heart.
Whose genuine self begins when labors close —
When with his friends, or books, or pen, apart,
His cheerful sunset light far round him glows.

X.

10.

FORGIVE — that thus the trumpet I have blown
You never sounded — never cared to hear.
The world, I know, can give no smile or tear
To those whose story it has never known.
But must the poet tune his lyre alone
To themes of passionate hope or love or fear, —
Or thoughts of loftier flight, yet shun the clear
Affection of two brothers' hearts at one ?
If gallant sonneteers may sing the light
And radiant demoiselles of olden time —
If in their melodies they may not slight
The fleeting passion of their youthful prime,
The old true loves from boyhood ever bright
Are surely worth the tribute of a rhyme.

SEVEN WONDERS OF THE WORLD.

XI.

THE PRINTING-PRESS.

In boyhood's days we read with keen delight
How young Aladdin rubbed his lamp and raised
The towering Djin whose form his soul amazed,
Yet who was pledged to serve him day and night.
But Gutenberg evoked a giant sprite
Of vaster power, when Europe stood and gazed
To see him rub his types with ink.   Then blazed
Across the lands a glorious shape of light.
Who stripped the cowl from priests. the crown from
    kings.
And hand in hand with Faith and Science wrought
To free the struggling spirit's limèd wings,
And guard the ancestral throne of sovereign Thought.
The world was dumb.   Then first it found its tongue
And spake — and heaven and earth in answer rung.

XII.

THE OCEAN STEAMER.

WITH streaming pennons, scorning sail and oar,
With steady tramp and swift revolving wheel,
And even pulse from throbbing heart of steel,
She plies her arrowy course from shore to shore.
In vain the siren calms her steps allure ;
In vain the billows thunder on her keel ;
Her giant form may toss and rock and reel
And shiver in the wintry tempest's roar ;
The calms and storms alike her pride can spurn.
True to the day she keeps her appointed time.
Long leagues of ocean vanish at her stern —
She drinks the air, and tastes another clime,
Where men their former wonder fast unlearn,
Which hailed her coming as a thing sublime.

XIII.

THE LOCOMOTIVE.

WHIRLING along its living freight, it came,
Hot, panting, fierce, yet docile to command —
The roaring monster, blazing through the land
Athwart the night, with crest of smoke and flame ;
Like those weird bulls Medea learned to tame
By sorcery, yoked to plough the Colchian strand
In forced obedience under Jason's hand.
Yet modern skill outstripped this antique fame,
When o'er our plains and through the rocky bar
Of hills it pushed its ever-lengthening line
Of iron roads, with gain far more divine
Than when the daring Argonauts from far
Came for the golden fleece, which like a star
Hung clouded in the dragon-guarded shrine.

XIV.

THE TELEGRAPH AND TELEPHONE.

FLEETER than time, across the Continent,
Through unsunned ocean depths, from beach to beach,
Around the rolling globe Thought's couriers reach.
The new-tuned earth like some vast instrument
Tingles from zone to zone ; for Art has lent
New nerves, new pulse, new motion — all to each,
And each to all, in swift electric speech
Bound by a force unwearied and unspent.
Now lone Katahdin talks with Caucasus ;
The Arctic ice-fields with the sultry South,
The sun-bathed palm thrills to the pine-tree's call.
We for all realms were made, and they for us.
For all there is a soul, an ear, a mouth ;
And Time and Space are naught.   The mind is all.

XV.

THE PHOTOGRAPH.

PHŒBUS APOLLO, from Olympus driven,
Lived with Admetus, tending herds and flocks:
And strolling o'er the pastures and the rocks
He found his life much duller than in Heaven.
For he had left his bow, his songs, his lyre,
His divinations and his healing skill,
And as a serf obeyed his master's will.
One day a new thought waked an old desire.
He took to painting, with his colors seven,
The sheep, the cows, the faces of the swains,
All shapes and hues in forests and on plains.
These old sun-pictures all are lost, or given
Away among the gods.   Man owns but half
The Sun-god's secret — in the Photograph.

XVI.

THE SPECTROSCOPE.

ALL honor to that keen Promethean soul
Who caught the prismic hues of Jove and Mars,
And from the glances of the dædal stars,
And from the fiery sun, the secret stole
That all are parts of one primeval Whole, —
One substance beaming through Creation's bars
Consent and peace, amid the chemic wars
Of gases and of atoms. Yonder roll
The planets; yonder. baffling human thought,
Suns. systems, all whose burning hearts are wooed
To one confession — so hath Science caught
Those eye-beams frank, whose speech cannot delude, —
How of one stuff our mortal earth is wrought
With stars in their divine infinitude.

XVII.

THE MICROPHONE.

THE small enlarged, the distant nearer brought
To sight, made marvels in a denser age.
But Science turns with every year a page
In the enchanted volume of her thought.
The wizard's wand no longer now is sought.
Yet with a cunning toy the Archimage
May hear from Rome Vesuvius' thunders rage,
And earthquake mutterings underground are caught,
Alike with trivial sounds.   Would there might rise
Some spiritual seer, some prophet wise,
Whose tactile vision would avert the woes
Born of conflicting forces in the state ; —
Some listener to the deep volcanic throes
Below the surface — ere we cry, " Too late ! "

XVIII.

THE FIRESIDE.

WITH what a live intelligence the flame
Glows and leaps up in spires of flickering red,
And turns the coal just now so dull and dead
To a companion — not like those who came
To weary me with iteration tame
Of idle talk in shallow fancies bred.
From dreary moods the cheerful fire has led
My thoughts, which now their manlier strength reclaim.
And like some frozen thing that feels the sun
Through solitudes of winter penetrate,
The frolic currents through my senses run ;
While fluttering whispers soft and intimate
Out of the ruddy firelight of the grate
Make talk, love, music, poetry in one.

XIX.

THE LADY'S SONNET.   TWILIGHT.

I KNOW not why I chose to seem so cold
At parting from you ; for since you are gone
I see you still — I hear each word, each tone ;
And what I hid from you I wish were told.
I, who was proud and shy, seem now too bold
To write these lines — and yet must write to own
I would unsay my words, now I 'm alone.
From my dark window out upon the wold
I look.   'Twas through yon pathway to the west
I watched you going, while the sunset light
Went with you — and a shadow seemed to fall
Upon my heart.   And now I cannot rest
Till I have written : for I said, " To-night
I 'll send your answer."   Now I 've told you all.

XX.

THE LOVER'S SONNET. MIDNIGHT.

I WAITED through the night, while summer blew
The breath of roses through my darkened room.
The whispering breeze just stirred the leafy gloom
Beyond the window. On the lawn the dew
Lay glistening in the starlight. No one knew
I did not sleep, but waited here my doom
Or victory. I saw the light-house loom
Across the bay. The silence grew and grew,
And hour by hour kept pace with my suspense.
Each rustling noise, each passing footstep seemed
The coming messenger I hoped yet feared.
At last a knock — a throb — a pause intense —
Your letter came. I read as if I dreamed.
Almost too great to bear my bliss appeared !

XXI.

THE PINES AND THE SEA.

BEYOND the low marsh-meadows and the beach,
Seen through the hoary trunks of windy pines,
The long blue level of the ocean shines.
The distant surf, with hoarse, complaining speech,
Out from its sandy barrier seems to reach;
And while the sun behind the woods declines,
The moaning sea with sighing boughs combines,
And waves and pines make answer, each to each.
O melancholy soul, whom far and near,
In life, faith, hope, the same sad undertone
Pursues from thought to thought! thou needs must hear
An old refrain, too much, too long thine own:
'T is thy mortality infects thine ear;
The mournful strain was in thyself alone.

XXII.

PENNYROYAL.

HEAVY with cares no winnowing hand could sift,
Wrapt in a sadness never to be told,
As o'er the fields and through the woods I strolled,
Following with restless footstep but the drift
Of the still August morn, so I might shift
The scenery of my thoughts, and gild their old
Monotonous fringes with a light less cold,
I found the aromatic herb, whose swift
And sweet associations bore me away
To boyhood, when beneath an oak like this
I culled the fragrant leaves. Crude childhood's bliss
Was in the scent ; but brighter smiled the day
For memories no cold shade could overcast —
Safe 'mid the unblighted treasures of the past.

XXIII.

BEETHOVEN'S FIFTH SYMPHONY.

THE mind's deep history here in tones is wrought,
The faith, the struggles of the aspiring soul,
The confidence of youth, the chill control
Of manhood's doubts by stern experience taught ;
Alternate moods of bold and timorous thought,
Sunshine and shadow — cloud and aureole ;
The failing foothold as the shining goal
Appears, and truth so long, so fondly sought
Is blurred and dimmed.   Again and yet again
The exulting march resounds.   We must win now !
Slowly the doubts dissolve in clearer air.
Bolder and grander the triumphal strain
Ascends.   Heaven's light is glancing on the brow,
And turns to boundless hope the old despair.

XXIV.

THE SECEDERS.

1.

FAR from the pure Castalian fount our feet
Have strayed away where daily we unlearn
How Truth is one with Beauty.   For we turn
No more to hear the strains we sprang to greet
When we were young, and love and life were sweet
Before the world had taught us how to earn
Its baser wealth, and from our doors to spurn
The Muse like some poor vagabond and cheat.
For we are young, and did not see the baits
That in the distance lured us down the roads
Where Toil and Care and Doubt, those lurking fates,
Subdued our pliant backs to alien loads ;
Till long since deadened to the Poet's tones,
They fall on us as rain on logs and stones.

XXV.

2.

YET what were love, and what were toil and thought,
And what were life, bereft of Poesy?
Who lingers in a garden where the bee
By no rich beds of fragrant flowers is caught —
A homely vegetable patch where naught
Is prized but for some table-caterer's fee,
And Nature pledged to market-ministry?
To me another lore was early taught;
And rather would I lose the dear delights
Of eye and ear, than wilfully forego ·
The power that can transfigure sounds and sights,
Can steep the world in symbols, and bestow
The free admittance to all depths and heights,
And make dull earth a heaven of thought below.

XXVI.

IN A LIBRARY.

1.

In my friend's library I sit alone,
Hemmed in by books.   The dead and living there,
Shrined in a thousand volumes rich and rare,
Tower in long rows, with names to me unknown.
A dim half-curtained light o'er all is thrown.
A shadowed Dante looks with stony stare
Out from his dusky niche.   The very air
Seems hushed before some intellectual throne.
What ranks of grand philosophers, what choice
And gay romancers, what historians sage,
What wits, what poets, on those crowded shelves!
All dumb forever, till the mind gives voice
To each dead letter of each senseless page,
And adds a soul they own not of themselves.

XXVII.

2.

A MIRACLE — that man should learn to fill
These little vessels with his boundless soul ;
Should through these arbitrary signs control
The world, and scatter broadcast at his will
His unseen thought, in endless transcript still
Fast multiplied o'er lands from pole to pole
By magic art ; and, as the ages roll,
Still fresh as streamlets from the Muses' hill.
Yet in these alcoves tranced, the lords of thought
Stand bound as by enchantment — signs or words
Have none to break the silence.   None but they
Their mute proud lips unlock, who here have brought
The key.   Them as their masters they obey.
For them they talk' and sing like uncaged birds.

XXVIII.

PAST SORROWS.

As tangled driftwood barring up a stream
Against our struggling oars when hope is high
To reach some fair green island we descry
Lying beyond us in the morning's gleam,
And shimmering like a landscape in a dream —
Yet waiting patiently the logs float by,
And all our course lies open to the eye —
So sorrows come and go.   What though they seem
A blight whose touch might turn a young head gray,
Joy dawns again.   Hope beckons us before.
The tide that pressed against us breaks our bars;
The visionary islands smile once more.
Life, with its rest by night, its work by day,
Forgets the old griefs, and heals their deepest scars.

XXIX.

LIFE AND DEATH.

1.

O SOLEMN portal, veiled in mist and cloud,
Where all who have lived throng in, an endless line,
Forbid to tell by backward look or sign
What destiny awaits the advancing crowd ;
Bourne crossed but once with no return allowed ;
Dumb, spectral gate, terrestrial yet divine,
Beyond whose arch all powers and fates combine,
Pledged to divulge no secrets of the shroud.
Close, close behind we step, and strive to catch
Some whisper in the dark, some glimmering light ;
Through circling whirls of thought intent to snatch
A drifting hope — a faith that grows to sight ;
And yet assured, whatever may befall,
That must be somehow best that comes to all.

XXX.

2.

Or endless sleep 't will be, — and that is rest,
Freedom forever from life's weary cares —
Or else a life beyond the climbing stairs
And dizzy pinnacles of thought expressed
In symbols such as in our mortal breast
Are framed by time and space ; — life that upbears
The soul by a law untried amid these snares
Of sense that make it a too willing guest.
So sleep or waking were a boon divine.
Yet why this inextinguishable thirst,
This hope, this faith that to existence cling ?
Nay e'en the poor dark chrysalis some fine
Ethereal creature prisons, till it burst
Into the unknown air on golden wing.

XXXI.

3.

If death be final, what is life, with all
Its lavish promises, its thwarted aims,
Its lost ideals, its dishonored claims,
Its uncompleted growth?　A prison wall,
Whose heartless stones but echo back our call;
An epitaph recording but our names;
A puppet-stage where joys and griefs and shames
Furnish a demon jester's carnival;
A plan without a purpose or a form;
A roofless temple; an unfinished tale.
And men like madrepores through calm and storm
Toil, die to build a branch of fossil frail,
And add from all their dreams, thoughts, acts, belief,
A few more inches to a coral-reef.

XXXII.

4.

Ir at one door stands life to cheat our trust,
And at another, death, to mock because
We thought life's promise good ; if all that was
And is and should be ends in fume and dust —
Then let us live for joy alone — the rust
Of ease encase our minds — the grander laws
Of souls be set aside.   Let no man pause
To weigh between his virtue and his lust.
From first to last life baffles all our hopes
Of aught but present bliss.   Death waits to mock
Our haste to indorse a visionary bond.
Let pleasure dance us down earth's sunny slopes,
And crown our heads with roses, ere the shock
Of thunder falls.   There is no life beyond ?

XXXIII.

5.

YET in all facts of sense life stands revealed ;
And from a thousand symbols hope may take
Its charter to escape the Stygian lake,
And find existence in an ampler field.
The streams by winter's icy breath congealed
Flow when the voices of the spring awake.
The electric current lives when tempests break
The wires.   The chemic energies unsealed
By sudden change, in other forms survive.
The senses cheat us where the mind corrects
Their partial verdict.   More than all, the heart —
The heart cold science counts not, is alive —
Of the undivided soul that vital-part
Her microscopic eye in vain dissects.

XXXIV.

6.

So, heralded by Reason, Faith may tread
The darkened vale, the dolorous paths of night,
In the great thought secure that life and light
Flow from the Soul of all, who, with the dead
As with the living, is the fountain-head.
And though our loved and lost are snatched from sight,
Some unseen power will guide them in their flight,
And to some unknown home their steps are led.
Yet has no seer, by sacred visions fired,
Disclosed their state to those they leave behind ;
No holy prophet, saint or sage inspired —
Save in the magic lantern of the mind —
Seen in ecstatic trance those realms desired :
And all the oracles are dumb and blind.

XXXV.

7.

The wish behind the thought is the soul's star
Of faith, and out of earth we build our heaven.
Life to each unschooled child of time has given
A fairy wand with which he thinks to unbar
The dark gate to a region vast and far,
Where all is gained at length for which he has striven —
All loss requited — all offences shriven —
All toil o'erpassed — effaced each battle-scar.
But ah! what heaven of rest could countervail
The ever widening thought — the endless stress
Of action whereinto the heart is born?
What sphere so blessèd it could overbless
With sweets the soul, when all such gifts must fail,
If from its chosen work that soul were torn?

XXXVI.

8.

NOT for a rapture unalloyed I ask.
Not for a recompense for all I miss.
A banquet of the gods in heavenly bliss,
A realm in whose warm sunshine I may bask,
Life without discipline or earnest task
Could ill repay the unfinished work of this.
Nay — e'en to clasp some long-lost Beatrice
In bowers of paradise — the mortal mask
Dropped from her face now glorified and bright.
But I would fain take up what here I left
All crude and incomplete ; would toil and strive
To regain the power of which I am bereft
By slow decay and death, with fuller light
To aid the larger life that may survive.

XXXVII.

TO JOHN GREENLEAF WHITTIER.

UNBIDDEN to the feast where friends have brought,
To greet thy seventy years, their wreaths of rhyme, —
For that thy form erect such weight of time
Should bear, was never present to my thought, —
Whittier, I bring my offering, though unsought.
Thou, first of all our bards, hast rung the chime
Of souls, whose zeal denounced a nation's crime.
Thy fire, intense yet soft, from heaven was caught.
Thou too the dear neglected chords hast wooed
Of plain New England life, and earned a fame
From whose wide light thy modest nature shrinks.
Long shall the land revere and love thy name;
Long find among thy songs the golden links
That bind the world in peace and brotherhood.

December 5, 1877.

.

XXXVIII.

TO OLIVER WENDELL HOLMES.   ÆT. 70.

A FOUNTAIN in our green New England hills
Sent forth a brook, whose music, as I stood
To listen, laughed and sang through field and wood
With mingled melodies of joyous rills.
Now, following where they led, a river fills
Its channel with a wide calm shining flood
Still murmuring on its banks with changeful mood.
So, Poet, sound thy " stops of various quills."
Where waves of song, wit, wisdom charm our ears
As in thy youth, and thoughts and smiles by turns
Are ours, grave, gay, or tender.   Time forgets
To freeze thy deepening stream.   The stealthy years
But bribe the Muse to bring thee amulets
That guard the soul whose fire of youth still burns.

November, 1879.

XXXIX.

BAYARD TAYLOR.

Can one so strong in hope, so rich in bloom
That promised fruit of nobler worth than all
He yet had given, drop thus with sudden fall?
The busy brain no more its work resume?
Can death for life so versatile find room?
Still must we fancy thou canst hear our call
Across the sea — with no dividing wall
More dense than space to interpose its doom.
Ah then — farewell, young-hearted genial friend!
Farewell, true poet, who didst grow and build
From thought to thought still upward and still new.
Farewell, unsullied toiler in a guild
Where some defile their hands, and where so few
With aims as pure strive faithful to the end.

    1879.

XL.

JOHN WEISS.

THE summer comes again, yet nothing brings
Of him but memories of that clear-lit eye,
That voice, that presence that can never die.
Fame o'er his dust no public trumpet rings.
No bard beside his grave his genius sings.
Yet he was one of that brave company,
The apostles of the race — the champion high
Of faith by reason guarded from the slings
Of dull sectarians and of atheist foes.
In him the scholar, teacher, prophet, wit
And genial friend were blended in one strain.
From his electric intellect arose
Auroral lights in which the past was lit,
And Æschylus and Shakspeare lived again.

XLI.

GEORGE RIPLEY.

WARM, generous and young in heart and brain,
A wise, ripe scholar of the antique mould,
Had he but chosen he might have enrolled
His name among philosophers who gain
Renown, and lead an academic train.
But unambitious in a humbler fold —
Humbler yet wider — he the current told
Of others' thoughts and works in graceful strain.
So from his watch-tower calm the public mind
He charmed and wisely led.   Still young in age,
And still in fireside talk the cordial friend,
He read between the lines upon life's page
The deeper meaning those alone can find
Whose souls toward truth and not its semblance, tend.

XLII.

TO G. W. C.

AUGUST 1, 1846.

THE day so long remembered comes again.
The years have vanished. On the vessel's deck
We stand and wave adieux, until a speck
Our bark appears to friends whose eyes would fain
Follow our voyage o'er the unknown main.
Shadows of sails and masts and rigging fleck
The sunlit ship. The captain's call and beck
Hurry the cheery sailors as they strain
The windy sheets ; while we in careless mood
Gaze on the silver clouds and azure sea,
Filled with old ocean's novel solitude,
And dream of that new life of Italy,
The golden fleece for which we sailed away,
Whose splendor freshens this memorial day.

August 1, 1881.

XLIII.

LONDON.

BLACK in the midnight lies the City vast.
Its dim horizon from my window high
I see shut in beneath a misty sky
Red with the light a million lamp-fires cast
Up from the humming streets.   And now at last
With lessening roar the weary wheels go by.
At last in sleep all discords swoon and die.
Now wakes the solemn visionary Past,
Peopled with spirits of the mighty dead
Whose names are London's glory and her shame —
Seers, poets, heroes, martyrs — deathless lives
Long blazoned in the chronicles of fame.
The inglorious Present veils its dwarfish head.
England's ideal life alone survives !

XLIV.

VEILED MEMORIES.

Of love that was, of friendship in the days
Of youth long gone, yet oft remembered still,
And seen like distant landscapes from a hill,
Clothed in a garment of aërial haze,
What need to sing ? Yet real is each phase
Of life ; and Time, that brings all good and ill
Of this our mortal lot, can never spill
One drop of that full cup he fills and weighs.
Ah, faces veiled that start from out the past !
Ah, spectral images once swift and warm !
Ye are but hidden by perspectives vast.
To-day o'ermasters all. And yet each form
Of life and thought, forgotten or aloof,
Is woven through the soul's strange warp and woof.

XLV.

TENNYSON.

1.

His brows were circled by a wreath of bays,
The symbol of the bard's well-earned renown —
Upon his head more regal than the crown
Of kings.   For he by his immortal lays
Is King among the poets of these days.
And far and wide where'er our mother-tongue
Is known, his wingèd lines are read and sung
In crowded cities and in green by-ways.
What could his country give that he had not?
Fame, wealth, love's best companionship he had.
And, blown across the seas, no lonely spot
Of our far West but felt the effluence glad
Borne to our hearts as from ethereal fire
In the rich music of his English lyre.

XLVI.

2.

How grand he would have stood, had he declined
The needless coronet he donned, as though
Its gilt could heighten his proud aureole's glow.
But downward he has stepped, a seat to find —
Not with the lords of that imperial kind
Whose simple manhood, fed by love and truth,
Found far from monarchs' courts perennial youth
In the ideal gardens of the mind ; —
But in a throng of blank nobilities
In outward fellowship of lip and eye —
Of empty forms and hollow courtesies ;
Thou art become as one of us — they cry.
Another shape than thine must now be worn.
Son of the morning — how thy beams are shorn !

XLVII.

TO G. W. C.

STILL shines our August day, as calm, as bright
As when, long years ago, we sailed away
Down the blue Narrows and the widening bay
Into the wrinkling ocean's flashing light ;
And the whole universe of sound and sight
Repeats the radiance of that festal day.
But for the inward eye no power can stay
The fleeting splendor of our youth's delight.
Still shines our August day, — but not for me
The old enchantment, — when, by care and sorrow
Untried, the hopeful heart was ever free
To greet the morn as herald of like morrow.
Yet shine, fair day !   And let my soul from thee
Hope, faith, and strength for life's dim future borrow.

August 1, 1884.

XLVIII.

GLADSTONE.

For Peace, and all that follows in her path —
Nor slighting honor and his country's fame,
He stood unmoved, and dared to face the blame
Of party-spirit and its turbid wrath.
He saw in vision the dread aftermath,
Should war once kindle its world-circling flame
Through Asian tribes that bear the British name.
Time few such crises for a people hath,
And few such leaders.   Calmly he pursued
A course at which the feebler spirits sneered,
The bolder fumed with clamor loud and rude.
And while the world still doubted. hoped, and feared,
This chief a bloodless victory hath won —
Britannia's wisest, best, and bravest son.

June, 1885.

XLIX.

J. R. L.

(ON HIS HOMEWARD VOYAGE.)

1.

BACK from old England, in whose courts he stood
Foremost to knit by act and word the band
Between the daughter and the mother-land
In all by either prized of truth and good,
We welcome to a fellowship renewed
His country's friend and ours.   The master-hand
That held the pen and lyre could still command
Affairs of state, controlling league and feud.
So, helped, not hindered, may his later strains
Flow deeper, richer, though by sorrow toned ;
And life by losses grow as once by gains ;
And age hold fast the best that youth has owned.
But ah, hurt not with touch too heavy, Time,
The light-winged wisdom of his gayer rhyme.

L.

2.

O SHIP that bears him to his native shore,
Beneath whose keel the seething ocean heaves,
Bring safe our poet with his garnered sheaves
Of Life's ripe autumn poesy and lore !
Though round the old homestead where we met of yore
In the unsaddened days the southwind grieves
Through his green elms, and all their summer leaves
Seem whispering of the scenes that come no more,
Yet may the years that brought him honors due
Where Europe's best and wisest learned his worth,
Yield hope and strength to reach horizons new
In the broad Western land that gave him birth ;
Nor bar his vision to a sunlit view
Beyond the enshrouding mysteries of earth.

June 13, 1885.

LI.

THE HUMAN FLOWER.

1.

IN the old void of unrecorded time,
In long, slow æons of the voiceless past,
A seed from out the weltering fire-mist cast
Took root — a struggling plant that from its prime
Through rudiments uncouth. through rock and slime,
Grew, changing form and issue — and clinging fast,
Stretched its aspiring tendrils — till at last
Shaped like a spirit it began to climb
Beyond its rugged stem with leaf and bud
Still burgeoning to greet the sunlit air
That clothed its regal top with love and power,
And compassed it as with a heavenly flood —
Until it burst in bloom beyond compare,
The world's consummate, peerless human flower.

LII.

2.

Shall that bright flower the countless ages toiled
And travailed to bring forth — shall that rare rose,
Whose bloom and fragrance earth and heaven unclose
Their treasuries to enrich, by death be foiled?
Its matchless splendor trampled down and spoiled?
Shall that Celestial Love — who watched its throes
Through centuries of long struggles and of woes,
And freed it from the old Serpent round it coiled;
Who tended it, and reared its glorious head
Above the brambles and the poisonous marsh,
And shielded it when zones were cased in ice —
Leave it to perish when the summons harsh
Of death is rung, — or, ere its leaves are shed,
Transplant it to his realm of Paradise?

LIII.

AUGUST.

FAR off among the fields and meadow rills
The August noon bends o'er a world of green.
In the blue sky the white clouds pause, and lean
To paint broad shadows on the wooded hills
And upland farms.   A brooding silence fills
The languid hours.   No living forms are seen
Save birds and insects.   Here and there, between
The broad boughs and the grass, the locust trills
Unseen his long-drawn, slumberous monotone.
The sparrow and the lonely phœbe-bird,
Now near, now far, across the fields are heard;
And close beside me here that Spanish drone,
The dancing grasshopper, whom no trouble frets,
In the hot sunshine snaps his castanets.

LIV.

IDLE HOURS.

YE idle hours of summer, not in vain,
To one by Nature's beauty fed, ye pass —
Though sending through the mental camera **glass**
No philosophic lesson to the brain,
But only pictures fair of shaded lane,
Of dappled cows knee-deep in meadow grass ;
Bright hill-tops with their sloping forest mass,
Or barn-roofs glimmering gray across the plain.
Earth, air, and water, and the sacred skies
Have something still to tell, not less, I ween,
Than famous books the learned sages prize,
Weighted with thought abstract and logic keen,
Where Concord pores with metaphysic eyes
O'er vasty deeps of the unknown and unseen.

LV.

MUSIC AND POETRY.

1.

SING, poets, as ye list, of fields, of flowers,
Of changing seasons with their brilliant round
Of keen delights, or themes still more profound —
Where soul through sense transmutes this world of ours.
There is a life intense beyond your powers
Of utterance, which the ear alone has found
In the aerial fields of rhythmic sound —
The inviolate pathways and air-woven bowers
Built by entwining melodies and chords.
Ah, could I find some correspondent sign
Matching such wondrous art with fitting words!
But vain the task.   Within his hallowed shrine
Apollo veils his face.   No muse records
In human speech such mysteries divine.

LVI.

2.

YET words though weak are all that poets own
Wherewith their muse translates that kindred muse
Of Harmony, whose subtle forms and hues
Float in the unlanguaged poesy of Tone.
And so no true-souled artist stands alone ;
But all are brothers, though one hand may use
A magic wand the others must refuse,
And painters need no sculptor's Parian stone.
If Art is long, yet is her province wide.
While all for truth and beauty live and dare,
One sacred temple covers all her sons.
Music and Poesy stand side by side.
Through every member one blood-current runs :
One aim, one work, one destiny they share.

LVII.

TO SLEEP.

Come, Sleep — Oblivion's sire ! Come, blessed Sleep !
Thy shadowy sheltering wings above me spread.
Fold to thy balmy breast my weary head.
Shut close behind the gates of sense, and steep
All sad remembrance in thy Lethe deep.
But come not as thou comest to the bed
Of the tired laborer sleeping like the dead
In dull and dreamless trance. But let me keep
The visionary paths of fantasy
Down through the mystic mazes of a land
Transfigured by thy wonder-working spell.
So lead me, gentle Sleep, with guiding hand,
That when I wake from dreams, I still may be
Wooed back to tread thy fields of asphodel.

ORMUZD AND AHRIMAN.[1]

A CANTATA.

Oh, that I could sinne once see!
We paint the devil foul, yet he
Hath some good in him, all agree.
Sinne is flat opposite to the Almighty, seeing
It wants the good of virtue, and of being.

But God more care of us hath had.
If apparitions make us sad,
By sight of sinne we should grow mad.
Yet as in sleep we see foul death and live,
So devils are our sinnes in prospective.

GEORGE HERBERT.

---

[1] I have here revised and enlarged a poem published some years ago entitled "Satan." The reader of the original text will find many important changes and additions in this its present shape — filling out and completing its rather sketch-like form. The new title too, I hope, is more appropriate to the subject than the old one.

THE OVERTURE.

Had I, instead of unsonorous words,
  The skill that moves in rapturous melodies,
And modulations of entrancing chords
  Through mystic mazes of all harmonies —
The bounding pulses of an overture
Whose grand orchestral movement might allure
The listener's soul through chaos and through night,
And seeming dissonance to concord and to light —
I might allow some harsh Titanic strains
  To wrestle with Apollo and with Jove;
And let the war-cries on barbaric plains
  Clash through the chords of wisdom and of love.
For still the harmonies should sing and soar
Above the discord and the battle's roar;
E'en as the evolving art and course of time,
  Amid the wrecks in wild confusion hurled,
Move with impartial rhythm and cosmic rhyme
  Along the eternal order of the world.

Then would I bid my lyric band express
In music the old earth's long toil and stress:
How the dumb iron centuries have foretold
The coming of the future age of gold:
How, ere the morning stars together sang,
Divine completeness out of chaos sprang

Through shapeless germs of lower forms that climb
By slow vast æons of a dateless time :
Till, through the impulse of the primal plan
They reach their flowering in the soul of man.

All swift-contending fugues — all wild escapes
    Of passion — long-drawn wail and sudden blast —
Weird, winding serpent-chords, their writhing shapes
    Shot through with arrowy melodies that fast
Pursue them, or that fall and lose themselves
In changing forms, as in some land of elves;
        The shadows and the lights
Of joyous mornings, and of sorrowing nights —
Strange tones of crude half-truth — the good within
The mysteries of evil and of sin,
Should weave the prelude of a symphony
Whose music voiced the world's vast harmony ;
        And only to the ears
Of spirits listening from serener spheres
Of thought, the differing tones should blend and twine
Into the semblance of a work divine ;
Where, not in strife but peace, should meet
What single were but incomplete.

I would unloose the soul beneath the wings
    Of every instrument :
I would enlist the deep-complaining strings
    Of doubt and discontent :

The low sad mutterings and entangled tunes
   Of viols and bassoons ; —
   Shy horns with diffident tones —
   The insolent trombones —
   The reedy notes
   From mellow throats
Of oboë and of clarionet —
Their pure and pastoral singing met
By clash of bacchanal cymbals, and a rout
Of tipsy satyrs dancing all about : —
Carols of love and hope checked by the blare
Of trumpet-cries of anger and despair : —
All differing mingling voices of the deep —
All startling blasts, all airs that lull to sleep ;
The mountain cataract that whirls and spins
   And bursts in spray asunder : —
Swift pattering rains of flutes and violins, —
   The tymbal's muffled thunder :
Æolian breathings wild and soft,
Notes that sink or soar aloft —
Soar or sink with harp-strings pulsing under : —
   Ravishing melodies that stream
   Through chords entrancing as a dream
     Out of a realm of wonder.

Or else, from off the full and large-leaved score
Into the willing instruments I 'd pour
A noise of battle in the air unseen ;
Of ghostly squadrons sending tremors strange

Of trouble and disastrous change
From beyond their cloudy screen ;
Low rumbling thunders — drops of bloody rain —
Earthquake and storm — presentiment of pain —
    Strange sobbings in the air
Hushed by degrees in fading semitones
    And softened sighs and moans,
As when a mother by the cradle stills
At night her weeping child, ere morn peeps o'er the hills,
And all the world again is bright and fair.
    While, with receding feet,
    Far off is heard the beat
Of mournful marches of the muffled drums ;
    And nearer now and nearer,
    Sweeter still and clearer,
The bird-like flute-notes leap into the air,
While the great human-heavenly music comes
Emerging from the dark with bursts of song
And hope and victory delayed too long.

So should my music fill its perfect round
With dewy sunrise, and with peace profound.

Ah, what are all the discords of all time
    But stumbling steps of one persistent life
That struggles up through mists to heights sublime,
    Forefelt through all creation's lingering strife : —
The deathless motion of one undertone,
Whose deep vibrations thrill from God to God alone !

PART I.

Daybreak.

CHORUS OF PLANETARY SPIRITS.

YE interstellar spaces, serene and still and clear,
    Above, below, around!
Ye gray unmeasured breadths of ether, — sphere on
    sphere!
    We listen, but no sound
    Rings from your depths profound.

But ever along and all across the morning bars
    Fast-flashing meteors run —
The trailing wrecks of fierce and fiery-bearded stars,
    Scattered and lost and won
    Back to their parent sun.

Through rifts of bronzing clouds the tides of morning
    glow
    And swell and mount apace.
We watch and wait if haply we at last may know
    Some record we may trace
    Upon the orbs of space.

Above, below, around we track our planets' flight;
    Their paths and destinies
Are intertwined with ours. Remote or near, their light

Or darkness to our eyes
A mystic picture lies.

First Spirit.

Close to the morn a small and sparkling star-world dances,
    Bathed in the flaming mist;
Flashing and quivering like a million moving lances
    Of gold and amethyst
    By slanting sunrise kissed.

A fairy realm of rapid and unimpeded sprites,
    That fly and leap and dart;
All fierce and tropic fervors, all swift and warm delights
    Bound and flash and start
    In every fiery heart.

Second Spirit.

Deep in the dawn floats up a star of dewy fire —
    So pure it seems new-born;
    As though the soul of morn
Were pulsing through its heart in dim, divine desire
Of poesy and love; — the star of morn and eve —
    Whose crystal sphere is shining
    With joys beyond divining —
Passion that never tortures, and hopes that ne'er deceive.

Third Spirit.

There swims the pale, green Earth, half drowned and
    thunder-rifted,

Steeped in a sea of rain.   Above the watery waste
Of God's primeval flood, all other land effaced —
     One peak alone uplifted.
The baffled lightnings play around its crags and chasms;
So far away they flash, I hear no thunder-spasms.
But now the scowling clouds are drifting from its spaces,
And leave it to the wind and coming day's embraces.

FOURTH SPIRIT.

Beyond, a planet rolls with darkly lurid sides,
Flooded and seamed and stained by drenching Stygian
     tides;
Deep gorges, up whose black and slimy slopes there peep
All monstrous Saurian growths that run or fly or creep;
And, in and out the holes and caverns clogged with mud,
Crawl through their giant ferns to suck each other's blood.
I see them battling there in fog and oozy water,
Symbols of savage lust, deformity, and slaughter.

FIFTH SPIRIT

I see an orb above that spins with rapid motion,
     Vaster and vaster growing —
Belted with sulphurous clouds; and through the rents an
     ocean
Boiling and plunging up on a crust of fiery shore.
And now I hear far off the elemental roar,
     And the red fire-winds blowing:
A low, dull, steady moan a million miles away,

Of whirling hurricanes that rage all night, all day.
No life of man or beast, were life engendered there,
Could bide those flaming winds, that white metallic glare.

Sixth Spirit.

But yonder, studded round with lamps of moonlight
  tender,
And arched from pole to pole with rings of rainbow
  splendor,
A world rolls far apart ; as though in haughty scorning
Of all the alien light of his diminished morning.

Seventh and Eighth Spirits.

Cold, cold and dark — and farther still
  We dimly see the icy spheres
Like spectre worlds, who yet fulfil,
  Through slow dull centuries of years,
Their circuit round the distant sun who winds them at
  his will.

Chorus.

Round and round one central orb
  The wheeling planets move,
And some reflect and some absorb
  The floods of light and love.

The rolling globe of molten stones,
  The spinning watery waste,

The forests whirled through tropic zones
By circling moons embraced —

We watch their elemental strife ;
We wait, that we may see
Some record of their inner life,
Where all is mystery.

A pause. The Spirits approach the Earth. The Sun rises over the Continent of Asia.

Second Spirit.

Look, brothers, look !   The quivering sunrise tinges
Our nearest orb of Earth.   The forest fringes
Redden with joy ; and all about the sun,
That gilds the boundless east, the cloud-banks dun
Flame into gold ; and with a crimson kiss
Wake the green world to beauty and to bliss.
See how she glows with sweet responsive smile !
    Hark, how the waves of air lap round her !
As though she were some green, embowered isle,
    And the fond ocean had just found her,
In Time's primeval morn of unrecorded calms
Hidden away with all her lilies and her palms ;
And flattering at her feet, had smoothed his angry
        mane,
And moving round her kissed her o'er and o'er again.

THIRD SPIRIT.

And now, behold, our wings are rapid as our thought;
And nearer yet have brought
Our feet, until we hover above the Asian lands
Beyond the desert sands.
There, girt about by mountain peaks that cleave the skies,
A blooming valley lies:
A pathway, sloping down from visionary heights
Through shades and dappled lights,
Lost in a garden wilderness of tropic trees
And flowers and birds and bees.
Far off I smell the rose, the amaranth, the spice,
The breath of Paradise.
Far off I hear the singing through hidden groves and
vales
Of Eden's nightingales;
And, sliding down through pines and moss and rocky
walls,
The murmuring waterfalls.
And lo, two radiant forms that seem akin to us,
Walk, calm and beauteous,
Crowned with the light of thought and mutual love,
whose blisses
Are sealed with rapturous kisses.
Ah, beautiful green Earth! ah, happy, happy pair!
Can there be aught so fair,
O brothers, in yon vast unpeopled worlds afar,
As these bright beings are!

CHORUS OF SPIRITS.

The stars in the heavens are singing
 Response to the wonderful story ;
Joy, joy to the race that is springing
 To cover the earth with its glory !

The race that enfolds in its bosom
 A birthright divine and immortal ;
As the fruit is enwrapped in the blossom,
 As the garden is hid by the portal !

DISTANT VOICES.

(A change to a minor key.)

Sin and weakness, misery and pain,
 Cloud their sunlit birth ;
And the sons of Heaven alone remain
 Gods unmixed with earth.

Light and darkness are the twins of fate ;
 Undivided they,
Through all realms that bear a mortal date,
 Hold alternate sway.

Through the universe the lords of life
 Never at peace can be.
Good and evil in a ceaseless strife
 Fight for victory.

Third Spirit.

I hear in the spaces below
A discord of voices that flow
In muttering tones through the air.
But where are they hidden — where?
There are trailings of gloom through the spaces,
  And far-darting cones that eclipse
The splendor of planets whose faces
Are dimmed by their darkening traces,
  And frozen by alien lips;
And the dream of a swift-coming change
Foretokens a destiny strange.

And what is yon Shadow that creeps
On the marge of her crystalline deeps?
On the field and the river and grove,
  On the borders of hope and of rest;
On the Eden of wedlock and love;
  On the labor contentment hath blessed?
That crawls like a serpent of mist
  Through the vales and the gardens of peace,
With a blight upon all it hath kissed,
  And a shade that shall never decrease?
That maddens the wings of desire,
  And saddens the ardors of joy —
Winged like a phantom of fire —
  Armed like a fiend to destroy!

SECOND SPIRIT.

Before me there flitted a vision —
　A vision of dawn and Creation,
Of faith and of doubt and division,
　Of mystical fruit and temptation:
A garden of lilies and roses,
　Ah, sweeter than dreams ever fashioned;
Hopes in whose splendor reposes
　A love that was pure and impassioned.
But alas for the sons and the daughters
　Of man, in the morning of nations!
Alas for their rivers of waters!
　Alas for their fruitless oblations!
The curse and the blight and the sentence
Have fallen too swift for repentance.
I see it, I feel it — O brother!
　It shadows one half of their garden.
O Earth! O improvident Mother!
　Where left'st thou thy angel, thy warden?
Is it theirs, or the guilt of another?
　Must they die without hope of a pardon?
What is it they suffer, O brother,
　In the red, rosy light of their garden?

THE SPIRITS.

Ye Angels — ye heavenly Powers
Whose wisdom is higher than ours —
From the blight. from the terror defend them —
Help, help! In their Eden befriend them.

The Angel Raphael.

Beyond the imagined limits of such space
As ye can guess, I passed, yet heard your cry.
For ye are brother spirits.   And I come,
Swifter than light, to shield you from the dread
Of earth-born shadows, and the ghostly folds
Of seeming evil curtaining round your worlds.
Yet can I bring no amulet to guard
One peaceful breast from sorrow ; for yourselves
Are girt about, as I, by that divine,
Exhaustless Love, whose pledge your souls contain.

The Spirits.

Ah, not for ourselves — but our brothers
  We plead, in their dawn overglooming,
For the death is not theirs, but anothers.
  Help, help! from the doom that is coming ;

For they stand all alone and unguided ;
  No Past with its lesson upholds them ;
Their life from their race is divided ;
  A childhood unconscious enfolds them.

Is it sin — is it death that has shrouded
  Their souls, or a taint in their nature ?
Is there hope for a future unclouded ?
  Tell — tell us — angelical teacher!

RAPHAEL.

Yon earth, which claimed your closer vigilance,
And seems so near to you in time and space,
Is far away.   Your present is its past.
To spirits, worlds and æons are condensed
Into a moment's feeling or a thought.
While ye were singing as ye watched those orbs,
They grew and grew from incandescent globes
Girdled with thunder, wreathed with sulphurous steam —
Or from the slime where rude gigantic forms
Of crocodile or bat plunged through the dense
And flowerless wilds of cane, or flapped like dreams
Of darkness through the foul mephitic air.
These shapes gave way to forests, rocks, and seas,
And shapely forms of beast and bird and man —
The last result of wonder-working Time —
Man — the tall crowning flower and fruit of all —
And the vast complex tissues he hath wrought
Of life and laws and government and arts.
All this ye knew not; tranced in choral song,
Your music was the oblivion of all time.

THE SPIRITS.

Have we not seen the approaching doom of Earth?

RAPHAEL.

The vision ye have had of joy and doom
Flashing and glooming o'er two little lives,

Is truth half-typed in legend, such as fed
The people of the ancient days, distilled
From crude primordial growths of time, when sin
Saw the fierce flaming sword of conscience shake
Its terror through the groves of Paradise,
Grasped by Jehovah's red right hand in wrath.

THE SPIRITS.

Was it a dream?   We saw that red right hand.

RAPHAEL.

The events and thoughts that passed in olden time
Dawn on your senses with the beams of light
That left long, long ago those distant worlds,
And flash from out the past like present truths.
It was a poet's dream ye saw.   It held
A truth.   'Tis yours to unfold the mythic form,
And guess the meaning of the ancient tale.

THE SPIRITS.

We mark thy words ; we know that thou art wise
And good ; and yet we hover in a mist
Of doubt.   Help us !   Our sight is weak and dim.

RAPHAEL.

Know then that men and Angels can conceive
Through symbols only, the eternal truths.
Through all creation streams this dual ray —

The marriage of the spirit with the form —
The correspondence of the universe
With souls through sense ; and that the deepest thought
And firmest faith are nurtured and sustained
By the great visible universe of time
And space — the alphabet whose mystic forms
Present all inner lessons to the soul —
And thus the unseen by the seen is known.
Yea, even the blank and sterile voids that span
The dead unpalpitating space 'twixt star
And star, shall speak, as light hath spoken once.

And hark ! Even now the unfathomable deeps
Begin to stir.   I hear a far off sound
Of shuddering wings, beyond the hurrying clouds,
Beyond the stars — now nearer, nearer still !

DISTANT VOICES.

(Confusedly. in a minor key.)

Behind us shines the Light of lights.
We are the Shadows. we the nights,
That blot the pure expanse of time.
And yet we weave the destined rhyme
Of creatures with the Increate —
Of God and man. free will and fate ;
The warp and woof of heavens and hells ;
    The noiseless round of death and birth ;
The eternal protoplasmic spells
    Binding the sons of God to earth ; —

The ceaseless web of mystery
That has been, and shall ever be.

THE SPIRITS.

Far off we seem to hear a chorus strange,
Rising and falling through the gathering gloom.
And now the congregated clouds appear
To take the semblance of a Shape, that bends
This way — as when a whirling ocean-spout
Drinks, as it moves along, the light of heaven.

RAPHAEL.

Spirit — if Spirit or Presence
   Thou art, or the gloom of a symbol —
   Approach, if thou canst, to interpret
Thy name and thy work and thy essence.

(*A pause.*)

Behold, the Shadow spreads and towers apace,
Like a dense cloud that rolls along the sea
Landward, then shrouds the winding shore, the fields,
The network of the gray autumnal woods,
And the low cottage roofs of upland farms;
What seemed a vapor with a ragged fringe
Changes to wings, that sweep from north to south.
And round about the mass whose cloudy dome
Should be a head, I see the lambent flames
Of distant lightnings play. And now a voice

Of winds and waves and crumbling thunder tones
Commingled, muttering unintelligible things,
Approaches us.   The air grows strangely chill
And nebulous.   Daylight hath backward stepped.
The morning sun is blotted with eclipse.

CHORUS OF THE SPIRITS.

Like the pale stricken leaves of the Autumn
When Winter swoops downward to whirl them
Afar from the nooks of the woodlands,
And up through the clouds of the twilight,
We shudder!   We hear a wind roaring
And booming below in the darkness ;
A voice whose low thunder is mingled
With waves of the sibilant ocean.
The clouds that were pearly and golden
Are steeped in a blackening crimson.
The spell of a magical presence
Is nearing us out of the darkness.
What is it?   No shape we distinguish —
No voice — but a sound that is muffled,
Muffled and stifled in thunder.
We are troubled.   Oh, help us, strong Angel!
A Form gathers out of the darkness,
Awful and dim and abysmal !

RAPHAEL.

Fear not the gloomy Phantasm.   Speak to him.
If he will answer, ye may learn of him

What human books of dead theology
Have seldom taught, or poets, though they sang
Of Eden and the primal curse of man.

THE SPIRITS.

Spirit, or phantom — darkening earth and sky,
And creeping through the soul in grim despair —
What art thou ?   Speak ! whose shadow darkens thus
The eye of morn ?

SATAN.

I am not what I seem.

THE SPIRITS.

Art thou that fallen Angel who seduced
From their allegiance the bright hosts of heaven
And men, and reignest now the lord of doom ?

SATAN.

I am not what I seem to finite minds ; —
No fallen Angel — for I never fell,
Though priest and poet feign me exiled and doomed ;
But ever was and ever shall be thus —
Nor worse nor better than the Eternal planned.
I am the Retribution, not the Curse.
I am the shadow and reverse of God ;
The type of mixed and interrupted good ;
The clod of sense without whose earthly base
You spirit-flowers can never grow and bloom.

THE SPIRITS.

We dread to ask — what need have we of thee?

SATAN.

I am that stern necessity of fate —
Creation's temperament — the mass and mould
Of circumstance, through which eternal law
Works in its own mysterious way its will.

THE SPIRITS.

Art thou not Evil — Sin abstract and pure?

SATAN.

There were no shadows till the worlds were made;
No evil and no sin till finite souls,
Imperfect thence, conditioned in free-will,
Took form, projected by eternal law
Through co-existent realms of time and space.

THE SPIRITS.

Thy words are dark.   We dimly catch their sense.

SATAN.

Naught evil, though it were the Prince of evil,
Hath being in itself.   For God alone
Existeth in Himself, and Good, which lives
As sunshine lives, born of the Parent Sun.
I am the finite shadow of that Sun,

Opposite, not opposing, only seen
Upon the nether side.

The Spirits.

Art happy then?

Satan.

Nor happy I nor wretched. I but do
My work, as finite fate and law prescribe.

The Spirits.

Didst thou not tempt the woman and the man
Of Eden, and beguile them to their doom?

Satan.

No personal will am I, no influence bad
Or good. I symbolize the wild and deep
And unregenerated wastes of life,
Dark with transmitted tendencies of race
And blind mischance; all crude mistakes of will —
Proclivity unbalanced by due weight
Of favoring circumstance; all passion blown
By wandering winds; all surplusage of force
Piled up for use, but slipping from its base
Of law and order; all undisciplined
And ignorant mutiny against the wise
Restraint of rules by centuries old indorsed,
And proved the best so long it needs no proof; —
All quality o'erstrained until it cracks —

Yet but a surface crack ; the Eternal Eye
Sees underneath the soul's sphere, as above,
And knows the deep foundations of the world
Will not be jarred or loosened by the stress
Of sun and wind and rain upon the crust
Of upper soil.   Nay, let the earthquake split
The mountains into steep and splintered chasms —
Down deeper than the shock the adamant
Of ages stands, symbol no less divine
Of the eternal Law than heaven above.

THE SPIRITS.

Shall we then doubt the sacred books — the faith
That Satan was of old the foe of God ?

SATAN.

Nations have planned their demons as they planned
Their gods.   Say, rather, God and Satan mixed, —
A hybrid of perplexed theology, —
Stood at the centre of the universe ;
Ormuzd and Ahriman, in ceaseless war —
A double spirit through whose nerves and veins
Throbbed the vast pulses of his feverish moods
Of blight and benediction.   Did the Jew
Or Pagan, save the few of finer mould,
Own an unchanging God, or one self-willed,
Who, like themselves, was moved to wrath, revenge
And jealousy, to petty strifes and bars
Of sect and clan — the reflex of their thought ?

The Spirits.

What if it were revealed to holy men,
By faith, that God had formed a spirit vast
Who fell, rebelled, tempted the race to death?
Whether a foe who rode upon the wind,
Or one within, leagued with some sweet, strong drift
Of natural desire, tainted yet sweet?

Satan.

Alas, did ever human eyes transcend
And pierce beyond the hemisphere of tints
That overarched their thought and hope, yet seemed
A heaven of truth? As man is so his God.
So too his spirit of evil. Evil fixed
He saw, eternal and abstract, whose tree
Thrust down its grappling tap-roots in the heart,
And poisoned where it grew; its blighting shade
By no sweet wandering winds of heaven caressed,
No raindrops from the pitiless clouds. No birds
Of song and summer in its branches built
Their little nests of love. No hermit sought
The shivering rustle of its chilly shade.
Accursed of God it stood — accursed and drear
It stood apart — a thing by God and man
Hated or pitied as a pestilence
O'er-passing cure. So hate not me. For I
Am but the picture mortal eyes behold
Shadowing the dread results of broken laws

Designed by eternal wisdom for the good
Of man, though typed as Darkness, Pain, and Fire.

The Spirits.

Must not the eternal Justice punish man
And spirits — now and in the great To-Be?
What sinner can escape his burning wrath?

Satan.

The soul of man is man's own heaven or hell.
God's love and justice will no curse on men
Or spirits, who condemn themselves, and hide
Their faces in the murky fogs of sense
And lawless passion, and the hate and feud
Born of all dense inwoven ignorance.
Man loves or fears the shadow of himself.
God shines behind him.   Let him turn and see.

[*Vanishes slowly.*

The Spirits.

Yet stay — speak, speak once more! Tell us what fate
Awaits the human race — now on this earth
Teeming with life — and in the great Hereafter!

Raphael.

The phantom-lips are dumb: nor could they answer.
The book of fate is known to One alone.

THE SPIRITS.

And thou — thou, sovereign Angel, knowest not?

RAPHAEL.

He alone knows whose being contains the all.
Cease questioning. Have faith. Love reigns supreme.

PART II.

A CHORUS OF HUMAN SPIRITS IN THE MIST.

FAR in the shuddering spaces of the North
 We live. We saw a Shape
Of terror rise and spread and issue forth ;
 And we would fain escape
The anger of his frown. We know him not,
 Nor whether it be he
Who claims our homage, for the shadows blot
 The sun we may not see.

We lift our prayers on heavy wings to one
 Who dwells beyond the sun ;
Whose lightnings are decrees of life or doom ;
 Whose laws are veiled in gloom.
Thick clouds and darkness are about thy throne
 Where thou dost reign alone.
And we amid the mists and shadows grope,
 With faint bewildered hope.

We fear thy awful judgments, and thy curse
    Upon thy Universe.
For we are told it is a fearful thing,
    O thou Almighty King,
To fall into thy hands.   O spare the rod —
    Thou art a jealous God !
O save us by the blood of him who died,
    That sin might not divide
Our guilty souls from heaven and Christ and **Thee.**
    And yet we dread to see
Thy face.   How can the trembling fugitive
    Behold thy face and live !

VOICE BEHIND THE MIST.

Fear not, for ye shall live if ye receive
The life divine, obedient to the law
Of truth and good. So shall there be no frown
Upon his face who wills the good of all.

CHOIR OF ANGELS IN THE DISTANCE.

God who made the tempest's wingèd terror
    And the smile of morn,
Who art bringing truth from sin and error,
    Love from hate and scorn ;

Lo, thy presence glows through all thy creatures,
    Passion-stained or fair ;

Saint and sinner bear the selfsame features
  Thy bright angels wear.

Human frailty all alike inherit,
  Yet our souls are free.
Giver of all good, it is no merit
  That we turn to thee.

Thou alone art pure in thy perfection.
  We thy children shine
But as our soiled garments take reflection
  From thy light divine.

Thou art reaching forth thine arms forever,
  Struggling souls to free.
Leading man by every good endeavor
  Back to heaven and thee !

CHORUS OF PLANETARY SPIRITS.

The presence that awed us and chilled us
Dissolves in the dews of the morning.
The darkness has vanished around us,
And shrunk to the shadows that color
The cloud flakes of gold and of purple :
So vanish the thoughts that obscured us,
The doubt and the dread of the evil
That stained the starred robe of Creation.
And we hear but one music pervading

The planets and suns that are shining —
The spirits that pine in the darkness
Or float in the joy of the morning.

SEMICHORUS I.

Have we wronged thee, O monarch of shadows?
  Have we named thee the Demon of spirits?
We know that the good and the evil
  Each mortal and angel inherits —
The evil and good that are twisted
  As fibres of brass and of gold —
To the All-seeing Eye have a meaning
  We know not — too vast to be told;
But the wise and the merciful Father,
  Though they stray in the desert and wold,
Will lift up his lambs to his bosom,
  And gather them into his fold.

SEMICHORUS II.

Yet the guilt and the crime that have triumphed,
  Though shining in purple and gold,
Shall bring their own sure retribution,
  As the prophets of ages have told.
For Justice is sure in the order
  That rules through the heavens of old.

VOICE OF A PROPHET.

Aye, though no tyrant's stern decree enforce
The law, yet Justice still must hold its course ;
Sure as the power that draws the falling stone,
Sure as the electric thrill from zone to zone,
The ocean's tides, the round of day and night,
The burning tropic sun, the winter's blight —
So follows, though long years have hid the seed,
The fatal fruitage of the evil deed.

VOICE OF A PHILOSOPHER.

Yet not, we must believe,
Like man's infirm opinion
And incomplete tribunals
God's larger judgments stand.
He sees the Past and Present ;
He knows the strong temptations ;
The nets where lie entangled
The creatures of his hand.

He knows the deep enigmas
No mortal mind has solved.
The armed and banded legions,
That bind earth's captives down,
Hold no divine commission
To pass the final sentence.
Heaven holds its perfect balance,
And smiles above their frown.

SONG OF HOPEFUL SPIRITS.

1.

Praise, praise ye the prophets, the sages
Who lived and who died for the ages;
The grand and magnificent dreamers;
The heroes, the mighty redeemers;
The martyrs, reformers and leaders;
The voices of mystical Vedas;
The bibles of races long shrouded
Who left us their wisdom unclouded;
The truth that is old as their mountains,
But fresh as the rills from their fountains.

2.

And praise ye the poets whose pages
Give solace and joy to the ages;
Who have seen in their marvellous trances
Of thought and of rhythmical fancies,
The manhood of Man in all errors;
The triumph of hope over terrors;
The great human heart ever pleading
Its kindred divine, though misleading,
Fate held it aloof from the heaven
That to spirits untempted was given.

CHORUS.

The creeds of the past that have bound us,
With visions of terror around us

Like dungeons of stone that have crumbled,
Beneath us lie shattered and humbled.
The tyranny mitred and crested,
Flattered and crowned and detested;
The blindness that trod upon Science;
    The bigotry Ignorance cherished;
The armed and the sainted alliance
    Of conscience and hate — they have perished,
Have melted like mists in the splendor
    Of life and of beauty supernal —
Of love ever watchful and tender,
    Of law ever one and eternal.

Song of a Wise Spirit.

The light of central suns o'erflows
    The unknown bounds of time and space.
The shadows are but passing shows
    And clouds upon Creation's face.
From out the chaos and the slime,
    From out the whirling winds of fire,
From years of ignorance and crime,
    From centuries of wild desire,
The shaping laws of truth and love
    Shall lift the savage from the clod;
Shall till the field and gild the grove
    With homes of man and domes of God.
And Love and Science, side by side,
    With starry lamps of heavenly flame,

Shall light the darkness far and wide ;
  The wandering outcast shall reclaim ;
Shall bury in forgotten graves
  Blind Superstition's tyrant brood ;
Shall break the fetters of the slaves ;
  Shall bind the world in brotherhood ;
Shall hurl all despots from the throne,
  And lift the saviors of the race ;
And law and liberty alone
  From sea to sea the lands embrace.

HYMN OF A DEVOUT SPIRIT.

The time shall come when men no more
  Shall deem the sin that taints the earth
  A demon-spell — a monstrous birth —
A curse forever to endure ; —

Shall see that from one common root
  Must spring the better and the worse ;
  And seek to cure, before they curse,
The tree that drops its wormy fruit.

For God must love, though man should hate
  The vine whose mildew blights its grapes ;
  Shall he not clothe with fairer shapes
The lives deformed by earthly fate ?

O praise him not that on a throne
  Of glory unapproached he sits,

For deem a slavish fear befits
The child a father calls his own.

But praise him that in every thrill
Of life his breath is in our lungs,
And moves our hearts and tunes our tongues,
Howe'er rebellious to his will.

Praise him that all alike drink in
A portion of the life divine,
A light whose struggling soul-beams shine
Through all the blinding mists of sin.

For sooner shall the embracing day,
The air that folds us in its arms,
The morning sun that cheers and warms,
Hold back their service, and decay,

Ere God, who wraps the Universe
With love, shall let the souls he made
Fall from his omnipresent aid
O'ershadowed by a human curse.   ·

SONG OF AN EVOLUTIONIST.

1.

All in its turn is good
And suited to its time ;
Fire-mist and cosmic flood,

Ice, rock, and ocean slime ;
Savage and Druid stern,
   Faith typed in legends wild.
The mills of God still turn ;
   Order is Discord's child.
Ever from worse to better
Breaks Nature through her fetter —
The spirit through the letter.
One vast divine endeavor,
   One purpose still pursued —
Upward and onward ever —
   All in its turn is good.

2.

Up from the centre striving
   Through countless change on change,
   Through shapes uncouth and strange —
The weakest doomed to perish —
   The strongest still surviving ;
   Purpose divine in all.
   Whether they rise or fall
Pledged to maintain and cherish
   Types higher still and higher,
   To struggle and aspire.
One vast divine endeavor
Upward and onward ever —
Through fish and bird and beast —
Power that hath never ceased —

Through darkness and through light —
Through ape and troglodyte,
Till best with best unite ;
Through melancholy wastes
  Of unknown time and space —
A power that never hastes,
  And never slackens pace
  Until the human face,
  Until the human form
  Beautiful, and swift and warm,
  Awaits the crowning hour,
  And blooms — a spirit-flower —
  Upward and onward ever
  One primal plan pursued.
  All in its turn is good.

SONG OF AN OLD POET.

I sang of Eden and Creation's morn ;
  Of fiend and angel, triumph and despair.
  I caught the world's old music in the air —
The strains that from a people's creed were born.

I soared with seraphs, walked with lords of doom ;
  Basked in the sun and groped in utter dark.
  I lit the olden legends with a spark
Whose radiance but revealed eternal gloom.

I stood enveloped in a cloud o'ercharged
  With thunder ; and the blind mad bolts that flew

Were heaven's decrees.   They spared alone the few
Whose hearts by grace supernal were enlarged.

Upon imagination's star-lit wings
  I flew beyond the steadfast earth's supports,
  And stood within Jehovah's shining courts,
And heard what seemed the murmur of the springs,

The streams of living and eternal youth.
  Was it a dream?   Hath God another Word
  Than that between the Cherubim we heard
When Israel served the Lord with zeal and truth?

Are those but earthborn shadows that we saw
  Thronging the spaces of the heavens and hells?
  Is there a newer prophet-voice that tells
The trumpet-tidings of a grander law?

The lurid words above the fatal door —
  The door itself — the circles of despair
  Are fast dissolving in serener air.
They were but dreams.   They can return no more.

No more the vengeance of a demon-god;
  No more the lost souls whirling in black drifts
  Of endless pain.   The wind of morning lifts
The fog where once our groping footsteps trod.

I looked, and lo! the Abyss was all ablaze
  With light of heaven, and not abysmal fire ;
  And fain would tune to other chords my lyre ;
And fain would sing the alternate nights and days —

The days and nights that are the wings of Time ;
  The love that melts away the eternal chains ;
  The judgments only of remedial pains ;
The hidden innocence in guilt and crime.

The sunlight on the illumined tracts of earth
  Sprang from the darkness, pale and undiscerned.
  And the great creeds the world hath slowly learned
Are truths evolved from forms of ruder birth.

The tides of life, divine and human, swell
  And flood the desert shore, the stagnant pool.
  And sage and poet know, where God hath rule
There is no cloud in heaven — no doom in hell.

Full Chorus of the Planetary Spirits.

1.

Hear ye, O brothers, the voices around that are swelling
  in chorus ?
Nearer and sweeter they rise and fall through the
  nebulous light :

Voices of sages and prophets — while under our footsteps
and o'er us
Roll in their orbits the worlds whose circles we
tracked through the night.

2.

Melting away in the morning, we follow their pathways
no longer,
Knowing the hand that has guided will bear them
forever along ;
Bear them forever, and shape them to destinies fairer
and stronger
Than when the joyous archangels hailed their creation
with song.

3.

Not with a light that is waning — not with the curse of
a dooming, ·
They shall accomplish their cycles through ages of
fire and of cloud :
Ever from their chaos to order unfolding, progressing,
and blooming,
Till with the wisdom and beauty of ages on ages
endowed.

4.

Out of the regions of discord, out of the kingdoms of
evil,

God in the races to come shall abolish the reign of
 despair.

Who shall confront his decrees with the phantoms of
 demon and devil?

Who shall unhallow the joy of his light and the health
 of his air?

5.

Lo! on the day-star itself there are spots that, coming
 and going,

Send through the spaces mysterious thrillings like
 omens of blight.

And the great planets afar are convulsed, as when winter
 comes blowing

Over the shuddering oceans and islands of tropical
 light.

6.

Shadows are shadows; and all that is made is illumined
 and shaded, —

Bound by the laws of its being — heaven and earth
 in its breath.

He who hath made us will lift us, though stained and
 deformed and degraded —

Lift us and love us, though drowned in the surges
 of darkness and death.

A POET'S SOLILOQUY.

On a time — not of old —
When a poet had sent out his soul and no welcome had
    found
Where the heart of the nation in prose stood fettered
    and bound
In fold upon fold —
He called back his soul who had pined for an answer
    afloat;
And thus in the silence of night and the pride of his
    spirit he wrote.

Come back, poet-thought!
For they honor thee not in thy vesture of verse and of
    song.
Come back — thou hast hovered about in the market too
    long.
In vain thou hast sought
To stem the strong current that flows from the Philistine
    lands.
Thou hast failed to deliver the message the practical
    public demands.

Come back to the heights
Of thy vision — thy love — thy Parnassus of beauty and
truth,
From the valleys below where the labor of age and of
youth
Has no need of thy lights ;
For science has marshalled the way with a lamp of its
own.
Till they woo thee with wakening love thou must follow
thy pathway alone.

We have striven, have toiled,
Have pressed with the foremost to sing to the men of
our time
The thought that was deepest, the lay that was lightest
in rhyme.
We are baffled and foiled.
The crowd hurries on intent upon traffic and pay ;
They have ears, but they hear not.   What chance to be
heard has the poet to-day ?

So we turn from the crowd,
And we sing as we please, like the thrush far away in
the woods.
They may listen or not, as they choose, to our fancies
and moods
Chanted low — chanted loud,

In the sunshine and storm — 'mid the hearts that are
   tender or hard.
What need of applause from the world, when Art is its
   own reward?